I0626355

ISBN-13: 978-1-7320501-0-5
Paperback
ISBN-13: 978-1-7320501-1-2
eBook

This novel contains characters discussing and contemplating certain methods of suicide, suicidal thoughts, substance abuse, and mental health. I hope it does so in a way which does justice to such a weighted, difficult subject matter with respect and responsibility. I also hope that those who have experienced such things will find something relatable and ultimately uplifting, and that those who haven't will find an understanding of and empathy for those struggling. If it's at all unclear in the novel itself, let me state this for the record:

If you are suffering, whether from mental illness or from the circumstances of your life or the social conditions around you, and you have had suicidal thoughts, I understand how you feel. You are not bad or broken for feeling this way. You are not insane for having these thoughts.

You matter.

USA, National Suicide Prevention Lifeline: 1-800-273-8255

Crisis Text Line: text HOME to 741-741

The Trevor Project: 1-866-488-7386

Trans Lifeline: 1-877-565-8860

Ophelia

Ophelia:

an american dream
by Aiden Blasi

Vermont

1

"You there?" he heard Her voice in his ear, a whisper crackling through the phone and crawling into his head.

He was still halfway lost in a hazy field somewhere just shy of consciousness. All he could manage in response was a low, blissful hum of affirmation that reverberated in his sternum, "Mhm."

He lay there for a moment longer. A moment that was utterly, completely, mind numbingly, deafeningly silent. She didn't speak. Even mostly asleep, he could feel the silence creeping down from his ears and through his spine for a few unending seconds. "Hello?" he reached out for Her through the phone.

And then he awoke.

Well, to be more precise, he didn't awake.

One moment he was in a dream and the next he wasn't. He couldn't have told you precisely where those moments were or what separated the two. But now he was awake. That he knew.

His eyes crawled open, and he took a moment to orient himself. He was in his room, between the familiar confines of those narrow walls. A sea of blankets and comforters enveloped him, shielding him from the chill. He loved the feeling of being cocooned in blankets, a bright side of his apartment being horribly not up to code.

He looked at his phone to see what had happened to the call, only to find that he did not have his phone to begin with. It was a small distance away on the carpeted floor on which his mattress lay, still connected to its charging cable and just out of arm's reach.

The cold pricked his bare legs and forearms as he slid out of bed, his boxers and off-white t-shirt offering little protection. He knelt down to look at his phone. It was 10:37 in the morning. Twenty-three minutes before he had set his alarm.

At this point he had realized that he was alone. That She was gone. Still, for some reason, he needed to check his phone, needed to see that there was no call in his logs this morning, needed to look at Her face in his contacts because he couldn't bring himself to erase Her. He sat down on his bed and called his voicemail. "One. Saved. Message," a robotic female voice announced. "June. Twenty fifth." A long, atonal beep as he felt his stomach churning and closed his eyes.

"Hey there," She said, Her voice light and playful, Her cadence bouncy. "Call me back, fuckface."

He shut his eyes tighter. But he could still see Her face.

He hung up the phone and tossed it aside onto the mattress before standing up and getting dressed. So much as throwing on a pink hoodie that violently clashed with his turquoise boxers can be called "getting dressed." Then, he opened the door to his room, the portal to the outside world.

Unfortunately, his world outside that room was a little less than 700 square feet, a one-bedroom apartment made into an impromptu two bedroom by the futon in what would be its living room. Currently, the futon was unfurled, but its occupant was sitting up against the backboard as if it were still a couch. As he was exiting the bedroom, he ignored the figure on the futon, sitting there with a bowl of Fruity Pebbles in his hands as a few talking heads shouted at each other on the television screen. A friendly "What's up, dude?" emanated from the couch.

The dude didn't respond as he strode over to the kitchen area and began searching through the fridge. "Dude?" the roommate called out again, his head still leaned back to look at the dude. "Preston," he shouted.

"Huh, what?" the dude finally responded, jumping up and turning away from the fridge, its door left ajar.

"I asked what's up."

"Oh, sorry, man," Preston said, turning his attention once more to the fridge. "Weird day."

"You just woke up, dude."

"Yeah, well..." his voice trailed off as he scrounged up a bottle of whiskey, a can of ginger ale, and a questionably old slice of a lemon wrapped hastily in plastic, then mixed the three ingredients over ice.

"Do you want to talk about it?"

"Absolutely not," Preston said as he poured the drink, more exhausted than angry.

"You're repressing your emotions, dude," the roommate informed him. "Not cool. Not kosher."

"Brett, you can't pull that psych major bullshit on me anymore," Preston sighed.

"Hey, dude, plenty of people drop out. Kanye West. Steve Jobs. Mark Zuckerberg. Julian Assange. Tom Hanks."

"Yeah, but-"

"Tom fucking Hanks, Preston."

"Well, let me know when you drop an album or... do whatever WikiLeaks does, or something."

Brett squinted. "Tom Hanks dropped an album?"

Preston shook his head. "Fucking idiot," he mumbled.

"Oh, I see, you're in a mood today," Brett turned towards his cereal and the T.V.

"I'm not in a mood."

"No, no, you are," Brett struggled to remain composed as he attempted to express himself. "You are in a mood to say hurtful and... and mean things, dude."

"I'm sorry," Preston said, a bite of annoyance in his voice.

"Are you?"

"Yes."

"Okay, thank you," Brett conceded. "Do you want to watch the news?"

Preston stood still for a moment as he took a sip of his drink and watched the screaming match. "I think I've seen this episode," he eventually answered before turning his attention once more to the kitchen and its contents.

"It's important to stay informed, dude."

"Yeah, sure," Preston said as he grabbed the jug of milk, a nearly empty box of Frosted Flakes, and a mostly clean bowl. "I'd just rather do it without all the, uh... You know, the... the theatrics and shit. I don't feel like getting worked up, man."

"Some things are worth getting worked up for. Like these uh..." Brett paused as a burp rose up in his throat, but he suppressed it to finish his point. "Like these assholes, you know, trying to take away our freedom and... bombing countries and shit. Real dick move."

"Right on, man, right on. Just not my scene, I guess. I'm gonna..." Preston motioned vaguely in the direction of his room with the hand that was holding his drink, while the other gingerly balanced his bowl of cereal in his palm. "Yeah."

"Woah, is that the last of the Frosted Flakes?"

"Yeah."

"Goddamn."

"Well, you should've gotten your own Frosted Flakes at the store. You got the Fruity Pebbles, man."

"I'm sorry, I thought this was a community," Brett shouted as Preston strode into his room and shut the door behind him.

Preston set down his breakfast on the floor as he lowered himself onto his mattress. From a sitting position he took a scoop of cereal followed immediately by a sip of the drink. Then, he slipped his phone and a set of earbuds out of his pocket and threw himself down onto his back. He took a moment to untangle the blob of wire and another to scroll through his music until he found the track that he was looking for, "Distant Solar Systems" by Julien Baker.

He closed his eyes. All his senses focused on the lingering bite of the alcohol in his throat and the wave of notes from a reverberated guitar that plucked on calmly but relentlessly, sending vibrations into his head that traveled throughout his entire body. All the while harmonized voices crooned and lulled him into a numb sorrow.

It was Her favorite song.

As the music faded out, he pulled out his earbuds and shot up. Then, he stepped over his breakfast to return once more to his doorway. He opened the door and called out, "Brett."

"What's up, dude?"

"I'm gonna go out tonight, you in?"

"Well, it's not like I got shit to do. So, yeah."

Preston responded by shutting the door once more and returning to his breakfast and his empty bedroom.

2

"So," Brett began. He and Preston were sitting across from each other in a booth, beneath a dim yellow light hanging from the ceiling. Preston's hands were wrapped around a glass of scotch and soda, while Brett's were combing through a small bowl of peanuts placed slightly off center on the table. He waited for Preston's eyes to meet his own through his thick framed prescription glasses. "Why'd we go out tonight?"

Preston shrugged. "Why do you ask?"

"Because," Brett proceeded slowly, "we're just sitting here, not socializing or anything. And I'm driving, so I can't even drink. I just gotta sit here and watch you drink."

Preston took a long sip. "I told you to get an Uber," he said when he came up for air.

"And I told you I don't trust Ubers. I'm not gonna get in some stranger from the Internet's car, my mom raised me right."

"It's the same thing as a cab."

"I don't like cabs either. Why do I gotta pay to trust a stranger with my life?"

"Well, you said it yourself." Preston took another long, deliberate sip. "Are you not entertained?"

"I gotta pee, dude," Brett said as he began rising from his side of the booth.

"Thanks for letting me know," Preston called out to him as he began striding away from their table.

Preston sat alone there for a moment. Soon he finished his drink and he was forced to sit truly alone. This he could only withstand for another few aching seconds, and after that slow and painful torture, he too rose out of his seat, taking his glass with him. He ambled over to the bar and leant against it for a moment, waiting for the bartender to come over. The bar was fairly desolate on this particular evening, so he didn't have to wait long before putting in his order, "Can I get another round of this? Scotch and soda."

"You doin' alright?" a voice suddenly interrupted as the bartender disappeared.

Preston turned his head to find the source of the voice that had annoyed him to a degree which surprised even him. He saw a woman sitting a few seats away at the bar, her phone and a martini on the bar in front of her, a book in her lap, her purse still strapped over her shoulder. "I'm good, man," he said, his voice almost hysterical. "You good? I'm good. Never better."

"I'm good," she answered calmly. "But you haven't been here long and you're already three drinks deep."

"You been watching me or something?"

"A little bit," she smirked.

"Well," he took his eyes off her as his next round came. "You haven't been watching too closely, 'cause this is my fourth. I think. Weird day."

She smiled at him while he took a sip. He began to once again become aware of the fact that he had never been with a woman before or since Her. "What're you reading?" he asked when he put the glass down. She lifted the book cover into his view. "*Sound and the Fury*," he read. "William Faulkner. Sounds exhausting."

"It is," she said. "Trying to get some more of the classics under my belt. Picked this up almost a year ago, still haven't gotten through it."

"You always read in bars?"

"Sometimes. I go crazy if I don't get out of the dorms every now and then. Plus, my roommate is a bit of a bitch."

"Oh, mine too."

"Are you still living on campus?"

He looked at her curiously. "No, I live in an apartment in the city."

"You do go to the University, right?"

"Yeah," he said between sips. "Do I know you?"

"We had a class together, freshman year. Intro to Web Development?"

Preston had no memory of the woman whatsoever. "Oh yeah," he said. "I remember you. Sorry, man, the, uh- the alcohol…"

"No worries," she laughed. "Honestly, I wouldn't be surprised if you didn't remember me at all. Seemed like you never payed attention to anything in that class except that girl you were always talking with."

And just like that, it was back. The hollow pain. The gaping lack. He was disemboweled at the bar. Now why did she have to go and say that?

"Yeah, right," he breathed, turning his gaze from the woman to his rapidly emptying drink as he ran his thumb over the rim of the glass.

"What was Her name again? Are you still dating Her?"

After another sip he realized that his lips were numb and he was swaying as if he were standing on a raft in a lazy current. "No, I'm not."

"Oh, cool. I mean, I'm sorry to hear that," she stammered.

"Yeah, thanks." He stood up off the bar and downed the rest of his drink, then set the glass down in front of him, along with a few bills that he fished out of his pocket. "I think I should be heading out."

"Oh."

"Yeah, I've been drinking a lot, and I need to drink some more, so I'm gonna go home... Nice seeing you again and all."

He didn't hear her response as he walked past her, looking back towards the booth where he came from. Brett had since returned to his seat and to his peanuts. "Come on, man," Preston called back to him. Brett stood from the booth, stuffing his pockets with handfuls of peanuts as he did so. He picked up both their coats and smiled at the woman at the bar on his way out.

He found Preston there, standing on the sidewalk, waiting, basking in the frigid night air. Preston began walking down the street towards their parking space, barely acknowledging him. "Wait, dude," Brett called out. "Who was that girl?"

"I don't know, some girl."

"Well, she was cute, did you get her number or something?"

"Nah."

Brett sped up his walking to pull up beside Preston and handed him his bomber jacket, though he seemed content enough to stroll through the dead of winter without it. "Dude, in my professional opinion-"

"You're not a professional anything, Brett."

"In my professional opinion, in order to achieve emotional closure, you seriously need to get laid-"

"Jesus Christ, Brett."

"I'm serious, dude, I'm just trying to help you."

They were walking up to the car now, a '98 Honda Civic, dull silver with a mismatched black front bumper. Technically, the car belonged to Preston, but the two roommates traveled together so often, and the car was so shitty that Preston was not particularly possessive of it, and it operated more as a communal vehicle between the two than anything else. The car squealed as Preston opened the passenger door. "I don't need your fucking help getting laid, fuckface," he slurred his words, throwing himself down into the seat. "Or getting emotional closure, for that matter. Fuck you, I'm emotionally closed."

Brett got in the driver's seat and took them away, the car bumping like a horse drawn carriage. A few minutes into their ride, Preston leaned onto his door and stuck his head out the window, feeling the winter breeze crashing into his numbed face and flowing through his unkempt hair. He remained like this for the rest of the ride home, appreciating the isolation. Half the time his eyes were shut closed as he listened to the ambient noises of the city streets that they traversed, the other half he gazed at the street lights and flashing signs for restaurants and bars that they passed one by one. He could taste the fumes from kitchens and grills lingering in the night air, he felt the dull, rumbling chatter of crowded city streets.

But all these dissolved away as they delved further and further from the city's epicenter. The long and arduous five-minute journey came to an end as the Civic pulled into its parking spot just in front of their apartment building. Brett could barely keep up with Preston as he stumbled and swayed with purpose into the building and the elevator. He and Brett spent a moment in silence in the intimate chamber, interrupted only by Brett saying, "Are you sure you're good, dude?"

And then Preston's exasperated response. "Yeah… Weird day."

The silence followed them. Immediately as they entered their apartment, Preston strode over to the kitchen and grabbed the bottle of whiskey they kept on top of the fridge. "I'm going to bed," he announced as he strode from the fridge to his bedroom door.

"Cheers, dude," Brett called out as he plopped onto the futon.

Preston closed his bedroom door behind him, a little harder than he meant to. A few uneven paces later, he fell into a sitting position on his mattress, leaning his back against the wall. He took a few deep gulps from the bottle. Then, he slipped his phone out of his pocket and felt the cool plastic of his case, the weight of the thing in his hands for a moment.

He unlocked his phone and tapped and swiped until he was on his contacts. He scrolled slowly, with dread. He got down to the O's, and then there She was.

He stared for a long time.

Longer than he knew.

Taking in the thumbnail of her in her gown from their high school graduation, the number he had long since memorized, her name. This was all that was left.

He lay the phone down on the mattress beside him, and he kept staring for a few more gulps of whiskey. Finally, he put the bottle down and took up the phone in its place. He clumsily pressed his thumb to the call button, a familiar motion. In fact, this whole process had become ritual in the last few months. Still, he felt his intestines doing acrobatics as the phone rang. His throat became dry and clenched nearly shut. He could hear his heart pounding between rings. He waited patiently for the voicemail, a generic, robotic female voice; She had never had the time or the energy to care for things like a voicemail message. Then the long, atonal beep.

Preston opened his mouth, but nothing came out for a moment. He closed his eyes. "It's me again," he finally began, and then immediately took another pause. "You know, sometimes I can't help but think that what you did was selfish and that you're a- a bitch for doing it. I know that's terrible. I… I feel like shit saying it. I am shit. But is it wrong? I mean, you had me, you had your family, your friends. How did you think we were all gonna feel?" He rubbed his face. "I get that you were in pain, but it's… It's not fair. It's not fucking fair.

"And I don't even, like, get that you're gone. I mean, I know it in my head and shit, but there's still, like, this gut feeling that you're here. Fucking months later and it's not getting any better. I'm… not getting any better. Sometimes… when I hear the door open, I… there's this- this… I don't know, this fucking instinct that maybe it'll be you. And I know it won't be. It won't ever be again. But I still get disappointed. Every fucking time. I know that's stupid, but…" He scoffed. "Sorry, I'm… I'm drunk as per usual. Just like last night. Just like every night… Just the same thing over and over."

He put the phone down.

The seance ceased. The night went on. He took a few more sips. Then he became frustrated. He hadn't said everything he wanted to. He didn't even know what he wanted to say, but that wasn't it; there was more. So, he picked up the phone and he pressed call again.

The phone rang.

And it rang again.

And it rang a third time.

But it didn't ring a fourth.

He kept waiting and waiting, but it didn't ring. There was only a thin crackle up to his ear. Then he heard breathing on the other end. His head pounded, sweat beaded on his forehead. "Hello?" he ventured.

"I'll give you a chance before I call the cops," a woman's voice said. "Stop. Fucking. Calling me. I don't know who you are, I don't know who you're trying to reach but it isn't me, so stop calling this fucking number."

The woman hung up and he was left staring down at his phone, Her dead eyes meeting his.

3

The following morning came as an abrupt, brusque halt to a deep, dreamless sleep for Preston. His alarm was wailing like it was getting murdered. His head was throbbing in pain. The light of the sun piercing through his window and landing squarely on his face was an obnoxious, authoritative visitor in his room. He rose to his feet, the blankets slipping off him to reveal he was still clad in the outfit of the previous day. There was a vague echo of pain aching in his entire skeleton, and his joints cracked in protest as he stretched out of his bed. The alarm was a deafening siren's call that he blindly stumbled towards until he finally crashed down on his phone and turned it off with bumbling fingers. Still, the pain lingered and reverberated throughout his skull.

He felt like shit.

While he had his phone in his hands, the memory of the call last night struck him like a brick upside the head wielded by a particularly disagreeable bricklayer, and he rapidly swiped to check his call logs. He blinked in the face of the bright, straining light of the screen. He had indeed called Her last night. Twice in fact: one time that went to voicemail, and another that was picked up and lasted twenty-three seconds. Every word spoken to him in those twenty-three seconds came rushing back to him. Every ring of the phone. Every inflection in the woman's voice on the other end.

And he had no idea what to do next.

He quickly scrolled through his phone once more until he found himself again on Her contact page, and he did a quick once over of the number listed there. It was Her number. The one She had scrawled on his palm in black sharpie when they both got their first cell phones in the summer after fifth grade. The one he had sent countless texts and calls to in the years after they reunited in high school. The one he had first called when he realized that he too was going to the University of Vermont.

And again, he had no idea what to do next.

He stumbled through his doorway and into the rest of the apartment, where once more he found Brett sat upright on the futon with a bowl of Fruity Pebbles in hand. "Good morning, dude," Brett called out.

"Yeah," Preston murmured, his phone still grasped in his hand.

"Hey, listen, dude." Preston strode over to the kitchen table and kept staring at his call logs and scanning through the rest of his phone for more information as Brett talked. "I've been thinking, and I think it's only fair that since you asserted ownership over the Frosted Flakes yesterday, and you yourself said that I picked out the Fruity Pebbles, that I now have the right to tell you not to have any of my Fruity Pebbles this morning."

Brett turned around and looked at Preston expectantly.

"Yeah, sure, man. Whatever."

Brett paused in shock and awe. "Really?"

"Yeah, yeah, it's cool, man."

"But… what are you gonna eat?"

"Huh?"

"Breakfast, what are you gonna have for breakfast this morning?"

"I don't know," Preston dismissed him.

"Are you still drunk?" Brett asked after a pause.

"No, no, I'm horribly sober."

"Oh." Another pause. "Look, dude, I wasn't actually gonna let you not eat breakfast, I was just using it as leverage to set precedent for a communal system, you know what I mean?"

"Brett," Preston snapped his head up. "I have more important things to worry about than fucking cereal right now, okay?"

"Are you okay, dude?"

"Uh…"

"Weird day?"

"Yeah, yeah. Well, more weird last night." He looked up from his phone once more. "So, I uh… I called Her last night."

"Who?"

"You know…"

"Oh," Brett nodded, "Her."

"Yeah, you know, I was… I was drunk and shit, but the weird part is that… Well, someone-someone picked up."

19

Brett paused. "What do you mean, like a ghost kind of situation?"

"No, man, I'm not talking about a ghost situation."

"Okay, good," Brett sighed in relief. "That is the last thing we need going on right now."

"The fuck are you even talking about?"

"Well, who was it?"

"I don't know, some lady."

"It wasn't Her is what you're saying?"

"No, it wasn't Her, what the hell, man?"

"And it wasn't anyone you know?"

"No."

"Are you sure?"

"She said 'I don't know who you are, stop fucking calling before I fucking call the cops,' so yeah I'm pretty sure," Preston raised his voice.

"Interesting, interesting," Brett mused. Then, he shrugged. "They probably just recycled Her number."

"Recycled it?"

"Yeah, they do it all the time, Channel 7 did a piece on it a few weeks ago. Someone got a new phone the other day, the company had Her old number sitting around, so they recycled it. You probably harassed some old lady who just finally got into the twenty first century."

Preston paused to absorb all this, then stuttered for a moment, which eventually resulted in the words, "So, what, Her number is just gone?"

"Well, it's not gone, it's just with someone else."

"But- but all Her stuff-"

"Yup."

Preston paused again. Brett watched him, waiting for his next words. "No," Preston finally concluded. "No, it can't just be gone."

"Sorry, dude," Brett said.

"It can't just be gone. It can't be someone else's."

Brett stared at Preston's soft, confused expression, and could offer only his most genuine and sympathetic shrug.

"That's-" Preston began. "That's all that's left."

For another moment Brett was silent. "She's never really gone," he offered up in a desperate final attempt. "As long as you remember Her, dude."

"But-" he cut himself off. "Do you think I should talk to her?" he abruptly asked.

"Who?"

"The woman, with Her number."

"Well, on the one hand, she did tell you not to call her and that she would call the cops if you did. On the other... No, there's really only one hand in this situation."

"I should apologize, though, right? That's the right thing to do."

"No," Brett emphatically shook his head.

"No?"

"No. You already probably scared the shit out of this poor grandma, just leave her be."

"She didn't exactly sound like a grandma."

"Are you seriously saying what I think you're saying, dude?"

"No," Preston recoiled. "Jesus, Brett. I'm just saying, you know, for the record. Just getting the facts straight."

"Well, irregardless of her age, dude, I say don't get mixed up in all this. Sounds like a whole lot of drama."

"I'm gonna call her," Preston decided.

"Put it on speaker, I wanna hear," Brett immediately responded.

Preston ambled over to the futon and sat on its end, staring at the contact in his phone the whole time. "Actually," he eventually said, "I'm gonna text her. That would be less... threatening, right?"

"Can't hang up a text either."

"Alright, alright." He stared at the keyboard for a moment. "What the hell do I say?"

"Well, start it off with a nice greeting."

"Dear phone lady..."

"It's not a fucking letter, don't start it off with 'Dear,' especially if you don't know her name."

"Do you have any ideas, then?"

Brett paused to think. "Salutations-"

"I'm not saying salutations."

"Why not, dude?"

"Because I'm not a fucking snake oil salesman in 1907 Wyoming, is why not, man."

"I think it sets a friendly yet formal tone," Brett mumbled, defeated.

"I'm just gonna say 'Hello.'" Preston typed as he talked and took long pauses to think between phrases, occasionally looking to Brett who offered a quick nod or a suggestion.

At the end of this process, Brett said, "Okay, read the whole thing back to me."

Preston cleared his throat. "'Hello. My name is Preston. I'm sorry for my voicemails, I realize that they must have caused you great distress and I'm sorry if I was at all threatening or irritating to you. Am I reaching you on a new phone? You seem to have gotten a number which used to belong to my previous girlfriend, who I was attempting to call when I left you those voicemails. I understand if you do not answer this or if you have already blocked my number by now, but I wanted to apologize and explain the situation to you as I think you deserve that at least. I will not reach out to you again except of course to answer any response you send to me first. Thank you and once more, I'm sorry.' I don't know, sounds a bit… formal I guess. Like an email, or something."

"Well, I'm guessing she didn't give you her email while she was cussing you out. And formal's good, show her you aren't always a drunken mess."

Preston nodded. "Right, right."

A pause. "Well?" Brett said eventually.

"What?"

"Are you gonna send it, dude?"

"Right… Right." He waited another moment before pressing the send button on his screen. His heart sunk with the quaint little swooping noise his phone made as the message was sent.

"There we go," Brett said.

"There we go," Preston agreed.

"Now we just wait. I'm sure she'll get back to you soon. Or maybe never. Who knows."

Hours passed. She did not get back to him.

Just before one o'clock in the afternoon, a time at which on any other given Thursday Preston would have gone to his class, he instead decided it would be best to stay in the apartment and relentlessly stare at his phone. Brett offered to go out to lunch with him, and Preston declined, opting instead for a peanut butter and jelly sandwich within the confines of the apartment. Brett was only slightly devastated.

The phone was suspiciously, maddeningly silent for hours. Every half hour or so Preston would scroll through his text messages even though the phone never gave its staccato, invigorating little buzz. He didn't dare place it out of his line of sight for more than a moment. He kept a careful eye on the battery, never letting it drop below twenty percent or so. He made a few fruitless attempts at distracting himself with a book or the television, but they did nothing to quell the rising anxiety that he felt dominating both his mind and his body. His stomach had become physically sick. The last time he felt this way was when he first started dating Her, and he was an insecure teenager that took every slight hesitation, every minute She didn't answer his texts as confirmation that She hated him and he was fucking everything up.

Eventually, Preston resigned to lying on his back on his bedroom floor, earbuds blaring music. As he lay, staring at the deathly still ceiling fan, fantasies and mirages floated in and out of his mind in a near constant stream. For a time, he merely observed the flow as the usual visions popped up and quickly dissolved: if She was somehow here again, how he'd wake up by Her side and they'd eat breakfast half-dressed before they went to their classes, and after they'd meet up to walk hand in hand downtown, talking about nothing in particular. And somehow everything was suddenly fine.

Soon, new fantasies came. He played out the conversation with the woman on the phone in his head, over and over, again and again. In one she was instantly understanding and apologetic. In another, it took time and some more explanation for her rage to be quelled, but she did eventually come around. Cold and indifferent. Kind and consoling. He played out every single word, as if he were writing a script, and it gave him a temporary consolation from the fact that for hours the phone remained utterly still.

In a few more hours, he emerged from his room and ate a mostly silent dinner with Brett. He only opened his mouth to confirm that the woman hadn't gotten back to him yet and to ravenously attack more cold leftover pizza. Once he had fully satiated his hunger, he sat on the futon with Brett and attempted to watch a bit more T.V., simply to hear another person's voice. But still his mind wandered to the unanswered text, to the fact that his one means of communion with Her had been ripped away by some stranger. He hated the woman on the phone, he decided. Not only had she taken the last piece of Her, but now she had the audacity to take such a harsh and cold approach to what was ultimately a simple misunderstanding that was no fault of his. He imagined her now as an irredeemable bitch, perhaps an authoritarian precalculus teacher or a member of a fascist party or a clerk at the DMV.

Beneath the chilled and at ease demeanor he kept, Preston found himself profoundly bitter by the time he returned to his bedroom that evening. There he spent a few more hours technically conscious, but not doing or accomplishing anything in particular, beyond stewing over the fact that the bitch had taken a whole day out of his life. It was around midnight that he decided, out of pure rage, that he would go to bed early.

However, as he was plotting this revenge, he heard it.

A brief but blaring buzzing as his phone shook on the floor across the room. He nearly dove out of his bed to grab at his phone and check his messages.

One new message.

From Her.

Immediately, he unlocked his phone and pulled up their text conversation. Her picture was there, with a small speech bubble next to it. New words. After he had spent the last six months agonizing and studying over every word they had traded that still lingered on his phone, new words had appeared. It was a simple, pithy message: "You really shouldn't be harassing your ex like that."

Preston studied the words for a while. The fact that she had used proper punctuation, spelling, grammar suggested a certain formality and a level of thought that starkly contrasted with the flippancy of its content: a single sentence in response to his open letter. A reprimand in response to his apology.

Judgmental and yet ultimately indifferent, he decided.

He began typing response, "well, not my ex, really." He paused. "She died." His cursor lingered for a moment and then he erased the last word. "passed away" he wrote. Again, he erased this, and then typed it out once more. He lingered a moment before pressing send.

The room was silent.

Almost instantly, a reply came in, "I'm sorry to hear that." He wasn't sure how to respond, even though he had heard the same sentiment over and over again since She left, so he was thankful when the second message came in mere seconds later. "How old was she?"

"She would've turned 21 two weeks ago"

"How long ago did she die?"

Preston was never sure what he expected, but it wasn't this. Her one condolence seemed like a mere formality, but she was at least somewhat curious. It seemed almost academic, her questioning. "july" he replied. Before she responded, he began typing again, "look this is just really weird getting texts from this number. would you mind if i called you? i think it might just help me process it all better to hear a different voice"

There was a pause, much longer than the others.

"If you think it will help." suddenly appeared on the screen.

Even so, Preston hesitated a moment before pressing the call button, just below Her face. And he hesitated before putting the ringing phone up to his ear and listening to the chirping. It rang three times. He could feel his heart pounding, rising in his chest. And then the ringing stopped. "Hello, Preston," a woman's voice immediately said.

So immediately that Preston was taken somewhat aback. "Hi," he responded. "You never told me your name," he realized aloud.

"That's right, I didn't."

He paused. "Well... Would you mind?"

"Dolly," she said after a brief silence.

"D- Dolly?"

"It's short for Dalia. Dalia Peterson."

"Oh," Preston scrambled to find a pen, flailing about on the floor of his room. He came up with a sharpie and began writing the name on his palm, saying as he did so, "Well you should just go by Dalia, if you don't mind my saying so."

"I do usually, in professional settings." Her voice was low and a little raspy. She spoke softly. Not in a meek or shy way, but a way in which she demanded that you pay her every word close attention. She didn't have a particularly identifiable accent, but there was a certain sophistication and quiet richness in her voice that set it apart.

"So, this is an unprofessional setting?" Preston joked.

She didn't laugh. "Are you the same age as your girlfriend?"

"Yeah, yeah. Twenty-one. I'm a junior in college."

"You sound older," she noted. For some reason it sounded like a criticism. "How did your girlfriend die?" she rapidly switched topics.

"Uh, She, uh... She committed suicide," Preston's voice cracked as it went low and he felt his throat closing up.

There was a silence. "Tragic," Dalia whispered, with a certain amount of sincerity.

"Yeah," Preston agreed. "Yeah, it was."

"What was Her name?"

"Ophelia."

"Really?"

"Yeah," Preston scoffed. "I don't know how that happened. Seems like Her parents were asking for trouble at that point."

"I suppose that makes you Hamlet."

"Guess so. I didn't kill Her father though, so there's that at least."

"Do you know why She killed herself?"

"You're awfully interested for someone who threatened to call the cops on me."

"That was before you had a story… Should I take that as a no, then?"

"There wasn't- there wasn't a note or anything."

"Interesting."

"'Interesting' is an interesting word to describe it."

"Well, some stranger starts leaving late night voice messages on the new phone I got for work, I tell him to fuck off, he texts me the next day with a sad story. A good story at that. It's got tragedy, romance, comedy in a twisted sort of way. Couldn't have written it myself. It's all horribly interesting, really."

"I thought it was just a coincidence."

"No, no, it's more than that."

"I don't under-"

"You have my interest, Preston. And my attention. What's your full name?"

"It's uh… It's Preston Carter. Why-?"

"Hmm… It's a good name, I suppose. Could be better."

"Thanks?"

"I'm going to call you again sometime, Preston. Within the next few days, probably late at night like this. You have my interest."

"Uh okay," Preston stammered. "Back at you."

"I assume this is your cell number?"

"Yeah, yeah, it is."

"Very well. I'll talk to you later, then. Good-night, sweet prince." Her last phrase was something almost resembling a joke, but her delivery was dry, deadpan.

"Good-" Preston managed to get out before she hung up the call.

4

Preston's eyes desperately scanned the contents of the computer screen, in which he could see his own frantic reflection in the morning sunlight. "Dalia Peterson," was scrawled in the search bar and at various other points across the screen. A surprisingly large amount of results had come up, bolstered by online bookstores, numerous literary reviews, even a few fan forums. "I'm telling you, man," Preston announced from his position on the futon. "This woman's on some Frank Ocean shit. She's some kinda big author, but she's got, like, no web presence. One interview that's like five years old. No Facebook, Twitter, Instagram, fucking Myspace, nothing."

"Is she good?" Brett's voice emanated from behind him. He was sitting at the kitchen table, eating a bowl of Ramen noodles for lunch.

"Apparently. She's some hot shit, man, according to these reviews."

"What was her name again?"

"Dalia Peterson."

"It's probably a… you know, a fucking, uh… You know what I'm talking about."

"No, I don't."

"You know, like a fake name, like Mark Twain."

"A pseudonym?"

"A pseudonym, dude, right."

"Mark Twain isn't his real name?"

"Nah dude, he's, uh, he's Sam-… Sam something."

"Huh. I wouldn't've pegged him for a Sam," Preston mumbled as he turned back to his search.

"What kinda shit does she write?"

"Uh, I don't know, man, nothing I've ever heard of. *The Congressman's Wife*, *The Homestead*, *West Coast Winds*, *To the Moon and Back*, *The Long Drive North*, *A Night in-*"

"Wait, dude, did you say *To the Moon and Back*?"

"Uh… yeah, why?"

Brett started laughing hysterically.

"What the fuck's so funny, man?"

Brett kept laughing, trying to calm himself down. "I know that book, dude," he said between breaths. "My mom had a copy of it." He kept laughing even harder.

Preston found his glee, to put it frankly, really fucking vexatious. "So, what's funny about that?"

Brett's laugh was incessant. "It's porn, dude," he eventually managed to shout.

"Porn?"

"Porn," he shouted again.

"What?"

"My mom was always really secretive with it, so I got curious and I looked at it once. It's fucking erotica, dude."

Preston paused. "Well, I'm sure it's not *erotica* per se-"

"It really is," Brett chuckled.

"I mean maybe it has, you know, erotic *content*, but that doesn't, like, detract from its literary merit."

"Dude, it's about this woman cheating on her astronaut husband while he's in space, and then he comes back and he bangs the shit out of her."

"Well, you know, that sounds like a compelling narrative, man. That's like the… human experience or something."

"The human experience of having rough, 'I-just-got-home-from-space' sex, maybe." He chuckled again. "You've been connected with a world-renowned erotica writer, how do you feel?"

"Fuck off, Brett," Preston said.

"Hey, dude, I'm not judging, everyone's gotta make a living, right? I'm sex positive." Preston just shook his head and dove deeper into his computer. Silence passed for a moment. "So, she's like a recluse or something?" Brett asked once he had settled down, though the ghost of a smirk still haunted his lips.

"Yeah."

"She live in a monastery or something? At the top of Porn Mountain?"

"Fuck if I know, man, I can't find a picture of her let alone where she lives." Preston shut his laptop with a firm slap and tossed it aside onto the futon. "I wonder if they have any of her shit at the library."

"Yeah," Brett scoffed. "They got porn at the library."

"Shut the fuck up, Brett," Preston said as he rose from the futon. He walked over to the kitchen table and scooped up his car keys. "I'm gonna go drive down there."

"Hey, would you mind picking something up for me while you're down there?" Brett suddenly asked.

"Yeah, what?"

"*50 Shades of Grey,*" he burst out laughing.

"Shut the fuck up, Brett," Preston called out again before the door shut behind him.

Almost immediately after he exited the apartment, Preston stuffed in his earbuds to avoid the silence of the long elevator ride down to the ground floor and the short stroll from the doors to the parking lot where the Civic slumbered. He hopped in the car replaced his earbuds with the car's aux cable. The speakers rattled on the passenger's side along with the bass, and he could feel the music vibrating in the car floor as he rode. The drive to the university was only about one song long, and he found parking quickly enough, surely a sign that this mission was god given.

He hopped out of the Civic, taking his phone with him and putting on sunglasses to bat away the mid-afternoon sun. He walked the campus for a while, at his usual leisurely pace, but with a certain newfound purpose and determination in his posture and his step. He reached the library soon enough, never stopping in his stride or acknowledging the rest of the student body around him, as he might have gladly done in a different time with different circumstances.

Once inside the library, he immediately went to the front desk, his sunglasses still perched on his face and his earbuds hanging around his neck. It wasn't long before a tall red headed man with a ponderous step and an even more ponderous personality came to the opposite side of the desk and smiled at Preston. "Hey, Preston," he said. "Good to see you. Missed Prehistoric Archaeology yesterday, huh?"

"Uh... yeah, yeah, man," Preston said, slowly sliding the glasses down and eventually off his nose. "I was, uh... I was sick."

"You didn't miss too much, don't worry. I can show you my notes later if you want."

"Yeah, that'd be pretty cool of you."

As the man smiled at Preston and assured him, "Anytime, man," Preston realized that he had completely forgotten his name.

"Hey, look man, maybe you could help me out right now. I was wondering if we've got anything by an author called Dalia Peterson here?" The ginger's face turned to a sudden slight grimace. Preston sighed. "It's for uh... It's for research, man."

The ginger returned the sigh as he shifted his focus towards a nearby computer. "That's what they all say," he said as he spent a brief second typing and then forcefully pressed the enter key. "Yup," he said after scanning the screen's content. "We've got a few of hers in. Third floor, romantic fiction section, under 'P' for 'Peterson.'"

Preston sort of nodded in gratitude and awkwardly shuffled towards the stairs. He climbed up to the third floor and ambled towards the romance section, acting as if he had simply happened upon it, looking over his shoulder for judging eyes every now and then. The coast was clear.

He browsed the section with greater attention, his eyes crawling across the shelves and down the alphabet until he saw Paklov, Patterson, Pell, Peregrine, and then finally Peterson. There was a sizable line of books standing in formation with her name scrawled on their spines. There were four of her books there, two or three copies of each. First in the row was *A Night in Rome*. As far as Preston had been able to find, it was her first novel. Though it received positive reviews at the time, the fan groups he had seen online largely wrote it off as a valiant but underdeveloped first effort, written before Dalia Peterson had really become Dalia Peterson.

Preston picked out the copy in the best condition and scanned the book jacket. "Intrigue. Lust. God. Hotel rooms," the summary proclaimed at him. "All these and more intertwine when an American dignitary is sent on a diplomatic mission to Rome, and her fate collides with that of a cynical, haunted cardinal of the Church-"

Preston quickly lost interest and flipped to the back of the book, inside of which was another small paragraph on the jacket. "Dalia Peterson is a young, up and coming author in the world of romantic fiction. Always seeking to push boundaries of artistic and social convention, what little work she has published, including a series of short stories in various publications including *The Atlantic* and *The New Yorker*, has already captivated national attention. She was born and raised in Los Angeles, California, where she currently resides."

He flipped through the first couple pages, and saw that her publishing company was also based in L.A. He rushed over to the most recent of her books in the library's catalog, *West Coast Winds*, which was published two years ago almost to the day. The same publishing company had stamped its mark on the first few pages of the book, with the same address in Los Angeles, California listed.

Preston scrambled around for a moment, grabbing one copy of each of her books that were in stock, and carried the small pile downstairs as stealthily as he could. At the front desk he laid the pile down in front of the ginger while casting a cagey glance around the room. Once more the ginger giant stared at him for a moment, somewhere between pity, disgust, and sympathy. His gaze alternated from the pile of books to Preston and back for a few seconds. "Are you okay, man?" he eventually asked.

"Yeah, man," Preston snapped. "Never better. I'm good. You good? It's research, man."

The ginger gingerly picked up each book by the spine and turned them over to scan the barcodes one by one. Preston gave him a forced, awkward smile after the last one was scanned, and he took the pile in his arms along with the following receipt. Then he did a sort of hasty power walk back to the car, gripping the books close to his side, careful to do so in such a way that the book covers were obfuscated by his arm. He placed them in his passenger seat and drove slightly above the speed limit on the way home, his gaze flicking back and forth from the road to the books.

5

Preston almost didn't notice the day turning into evening and then into night or the fact that his phone barely moved during that time. He was shut in his room, sitting on the floor with his back against the wall, the books that he had checked out sitting next to him. He had *A Night in Rome* open in his hands, already a few hundred pages deep into the thing, even though he was not particularly interested in the story itself. He was, however, enthralled with every word that Dalia put on the page, regardless of what she was writing about.

And so, the only thing that broke his focus from the novel in front of him was the buzzing of his phone as it lit up and cast a ray of pure white light into the dimly lit room. Instantly, he put the book down and looked at the nearly blinding screen. "Ophelia Lawson," was written at the top of the screen, above a picture of her smiling face.

His stomach plunged as he accepted the call. "Hello?" he reached out.

"Hello, Preston, it's me, Dalia." For some reason, Preston was half surprised it wasn't Her. "Is this a good time?"

"Uh, yeah, it's fine. I was just… reading."

She didn't show any curiosity in what he was reading, as he hoped she would. "I'm sorry to have to call you so late, but this really is the only time I have to myself," she said.

"Oh, don't worry about it. I'm a night person, anyway." Before she got a chance to continue, Preston interjected, "So, I was reading one of *your* books actually."

"Oh, really," she feigned interest poorly. "Which one?"

"Uh, *Night in Rome.*"

"Ugh, you really shouldn't have started with that one."

"I think it's pretty good."

"It's derivative, uninspired, if we're being perfectly honest with ourselves. I was young. I was so proud of it at the time, but I cringe at some of it now." Preston opened his mouth to object, but this time it was Dalia's turn to interject. "Enough about that. Let's get down to business."

"Right, business… What exactly is our business?"

"Well, I suppose it's not really business, per se. I'm simply… intrigued. Aren't you?"

"Yeah, I guess so."

"Well there you have it, then. We'll explore this little intrigue." There was a long, palpable silence between them. "So…" she began.

"So."

"Tell me about Her."

Preston sighed through his nose. "What do you want to know?"

Dalia paused for a moment. "I know you said there wasn't a note, but surely you must know on some level why She-"

"Jesus, you're just jumping right into it, aren't you?"

"I'm sorry to be blunt, but-"

"Why are you giving me the fucking third degree here?" Preston realized he had raised his voice.

Again, Dalia paused, and returned with a calm, enchanting voice. "Because you have a good story. I'm not trying to interrogate you, I just want to hear your story."

"Of course, why wouldn't I want to be your bed time story?"

"To me, you're a total stranger. Someone who I imagine I would have never met if not for a coincidence that occurred at incalculable odds. I don't know you and you don't know me. I doubt that we ever will in the traditional sense. But there's a kind of intimacy in that, don't you think? And it's a dying kind of intimacy these days. I imagine, for instance, that you were reading my book because you spent some time Googling me, knowing that if I allowed you to, as most people do, you could know everything about me there is to know." Preston shifted uncomfortably in his seat. "Sometimes we need strangers, don't we?"

"I'd still like to know you better."

"You know my name. You know my work. I imagine you know that I live in Los Angeles. Do you really need more than that?"

"If I'm going to be talking to you about shit like this, then yeah."

"Isn't it liberating though? Talking to a complete stranger."

"What do you mean?"

"Well, have you ever talked to anyone about what happened? Really talked, I mean."

Preston paused. There had to be someone. There was the counselor that the school brought in and "strongly encouraged" that he meet with, but he barely said a word. He remembered just staring at the hardwood floors, nodding along to what the man was saying without really listening, running his fingertips over the edge of the armrest of his leather couch, picking at a crack through which thin wisps of cotton were exposed. "No," he finally answered. "It's funny, people kept offering, but I knew they never meant it. I knew they were all desperately hoping I wouldn't actually try. Even if they did mean it, how could they possibly... know, you know?"

"Those were all people you knew in reality. People who were just trying to seem nice, trying to make you feel better without actually doing anything. They were obligated to offer something because they knew you, because they pitied you. There's none of that with me. I'm genuinely interested. And I can just tell you the truth. And you can tell me the truth. Because there are no consequences. This is an opportunity for you here, don't you want to take advantage of it?"

"Yeah… Yeah, I guess."

"Well, I'll start again then… How've you been doing?"

"Oh… As good as you can expect, I guess."

"Preston," she pressed.

"What?"

"That doesn't mean anything."

"No, it doesn't, I guess. But that's what everyone keeps saying about me, so I don't know. But… I don't know. I don't- I don't feel good."

"Understandable, I suppose."

"Yeah, yeah, I guess so. But there's some- I don't know, some weird stuff to it."

"Like what?"

"I just mean, like, stuff you wouldn't think of." Dalia silently demanded elaboration. "Well… It's like, just after it happened, everything became a first again. Like there's just two eras now, before Her and after Her. For a while after, it was just like 'Oh, this is the first time I'm taking out the trash since She died. I think that tissue was Hers.' Or like, 'After I do this load of laundry, this hoodie's not gonna smell like her ever again.' And then I'm getting all fucking worked up because my roommate cleaned the shower drain and there isn't any of Her hair in it anymore." He scratched his head. "My hair is super fucking long right now because I just can't bring myself to get my first haircut, for some reason. She always liked it after a fresh cut."

"You can't admit that life is moving on without Her," Dalia said.

This time it was Preston who took a lengthy pause. He had never quite heard it put into words.

He had never heard himself say those words out loud and now they were just pouring out of him like blood out of a wound. "I lied earlier," he said.

"About what?"

"I- I know why She killed Herself. At least, I think that I know. There were a lot of reasons, really."

"I can't imagine suicide is ever really a simple matter."

"Not in my experience... She was smart. She was really fucking smart. Smart doesn't even... begin to describe Her. She was wise, you know? She just always had this air about her like She was just on a higher plane than everyone else. Sometimes it was hard to tell when She was... being that or when She was just... gone, though."

"She was..." Dalia for once couldn't find the right word.

"She had good days and bad days. I remember in elementary school they said She was 'creative' and 'full of imagination,'" he scoffed. "Most of the time She had a handle on everything though, She wasn't... delusional or anything like that. Emotionally, She was..."

"Volatile?"

"Yeah, yeah. That's the word. Volatile." Preston's eyes wandered down to stare beyond the floor and he combed the carpet with his fingertips. "Sometimes we would go weeks, months and everything was amazing the whole time. But for every one of those, there was a week of fighting, just screaming all the time, or a week where She just couldn't bring herself to get out of bed."

"You said you knew Her in elementary school?"

"Yeah. She was my first crush. Then She moved out to California cause Her dad got a job out there, then Her parents split so She and Her mom moved back when we started high school and we became friends again. Started dating the summer after senior year, up until... Well, you know. Almost three years."

"Did you love Her?"

"Yeah," he sighed heavily. He shut his eyes and threw his head back. "Yeah, I did. I fell fucking head over heels from the beginning. It still feels like yesterday when we first kissed. We had been on a date that I didn't really know was a date until She dropped me off on my porch and kissed me at the last second, and then She literally ran away right after."

Dalia laughed. It was the first time he had heard her laugh, a low, subtle melody that made him instantly want to hear it again. "She was shy, then?"

"Sometimes. Most of the time She was... She was the life of wherever She was, you know. But She was always sort of insecure. Self-loathing. She had some real trust issues. She was always paranoid that I didn't love Her, that I was cheating on Her, that I was gonna abandon Her."

"Any particular reason why?"

"I don't really know. I'm not a therapist, but I'm guessing Her whole childhood didn't really help. Her dad... He was a real piece of shit. I didn't even get to know the specifics of some of the shit he did to Her."

"Do you think it was that self-loathing that did it?"

"In part, probably. On a deep-down level, you know. And it probably didn't help when drugs came into the mix. Serious shit. Some of the shit I hadn't even heard of before."

"That never helps."

"Yeah, well… For some, probably most people, it's all mostly fine. She was always… I don't know how to describe it. Dissociation was the word the doctors kept using."

"So, what, She… didn't have a grasp on reality?"

"There were moments before where She felt like She wasn't real, but that was all kinda mild stuff, maybe threw Her off for a day at most. But at the end, it was different. I think-" He let another long pause pass as he stared into the night. "I think She thought She was dreaming." Dalia was silent. He wondered if she didn't know what to say. "Her mom found Her in the bathtub… under the water, couple empty bottles of pills on the floor. I woke up a few hours later with forty-seven missed calls and the police knocking on my door. It's funny, because *that* didn't feel real. It still doesn't really. I keep thinking that I'm just about to wake up next to Her and I can just tell Her all about this shitty nightmare I had and I'll be back in one of the good days. But I never wake up."

"Are you going to hurt yourself, Preston?"

"I've thought about it. A lot. But no."

"Good." She paused for a moment. "Can I ask you something?" she whispered.

"We've already come this far."

"On the phone, when you still thought this was Her number..." Preston cringed at the memory. "You called Her selfish."

"I was... drunk."

"I know, but... Is that how you really felt?"

He gulped. "I- It's kinda hard not to feel that way sometimes, you know? I just- I don't understand how She could just... abandon me like that."

"When I was fourteen," Dalia suddenly began, "I tried to hang myself with a belt from the ceiling fan in my room. When I fell, it jolted my whole body, but it wasn't quite enough to break my neck. So, I just dangled there for a while." Her voice was low, even, eerily serene. "I was completely panicking, despite it all. Totally terrified. Every single primal instinct in a human body tells you to survive. To defy that, to try and take your own life, it never feels good, it never feels natural. I was kicking and flailing everywhere. I remember feeling the carpet grazing my toes, just out of reach. I felt my pulse pounding in my ears faster and faster and faster, and I kept opening my mouth and gasping but I just couldn't get any air. There was this pressure building up in my lungs like they were about to burst.

"Then... the belt broke. The buckle snapped. I just kind of laid there on the ground. Breathing. Running my fingers through the carpet. After a few minutes, I got up, and I wore a scarf to cover the bruises, and I went to school, and I just carried on. I never told anyone about that until now. You're the only one who knows."

"Wow," was all Preston could manage.

"I guess what I'm trying to say is that there aren't many people who really want to die. They just carry this weight with them all their lives until they reach their breaking point and there's only one way to get rid of the pain."

"But… That's the thing. She didn't get rid of any pain, She just dumped it on my lap and on everyone else that cared about Her."

"She knew that. She knew that people would suffer because of what She did. And She still couldn't find another way out… Did you ever hear about the… Triangle Shirtwaist Factory fire?"

"Uh…" Preston's eyes shifted around the room in confusion. "You're taking me back to my history class in sophomore year of high school, but yeah. I think I know what you mean."

"There were over a hundred deaths, and maybe half of them came from people jumping off the building. Can you imagine? Looking down from a window, at a hundred-foot drop onto concrete and asphalt. There's nothing ahead of you but that straight drop, but behind you is even worse. There's that warmth on your back and the cloud of smoke that's drifting out the window, filling your lungs, and you know that if you don't do something the fire's gonna swallow you whole. Those people were under no illusions. They didn't jump because they thought they could escape. They jumped because the alternative was to burn." There was a long, drawn out silence. "That's about the best way I can describe it, I think."

"I-... I guess I never really thought of it like that."

"I'm going to keep calling you, Preston. I hope that at least gives you something to look forward to."

"I think so," he muttered.

"Are you alright?"

"Yeah," he croaked. "Yeah," he repeated, more resolutely, nodding to himself.

"Do you want to tell me anything else, Preston?"

"I guess not." His mumble returned, his words even more indistinct. In truth, he did want to tell her more, but he couldn't think of anything else to say. "I'm tired."

"I understand," she stated. "Goodnight, Preston."

"Goodnight, Dalia."

He didn't really want to hear the dim, bubbly bloop his phone sang when a call ended. He knew what came after it. A hollow pain in his chest. A vague malaise. A profound emptiness. Utter numbness. Loneliness, with the knowledge that no matter how many people, bottles, books, drugs he surrounded himself with, he wouldn't feel any less alone. Maybe he never would. This was the worst he had felt it since the very moment that two officers knocked on his door and told him something he couldn't possibly comprehend.

6

In the following days, Preston decided that he probably should in fact attend his classes, however it was ultimately some fruitless shit. He couldn't pay attention to anything for more than a few moments. He felt half-awake through the entire day. His eyes kept flickering towards his phone, hoping that he would see Dalia calling him there, under the pseudonym of Ophelia, even though he knew their communions were strictly a ritual left for the late nights. When he wasn't scanning his phone, he was mentally writing his script for what he would say the next time that she called him, picking out the playlist of traumas he would share with her that night. Occasionally, he felt an urge to call her first or at least send her a text, but he could always talk himself out of it for fear that he would be clinging too tight. But he couldn't let her slip through his fingers either.

He had gone through the four books of hers that were in stock at the library in two weeks, an endeavor far more important than petty things like school work and having a social life. The basic extent of his human interactions outside of his classes and his appointments with Dalia was when Brett would knock on his bedroom door and cautiously enter, starting a dialogue that varied little from day to day. "How you doing, dude?" Brett would ask, or something to that effect.

"I'm fine, Brett," Preston would answer.

"You sure, dude?"

"Yeah."

"How's the book?"

"Oh, you know, it's pretty good."

"Okay, dude."

Brett would then linger in the door frame a moment longer before uttering something about how he was there if Preston ever needed anything. Preston would answer thankfully, half sincerely.

Perhaps that's why during one of these phone calls, after discussing at length the last book he had read, Preston felt compelled to blurt out, "You know, I'm glad that you ended up being a woman."

"Well, the whole period thing and the sexism is bit of a drag, but I would say it's treated me alright so far."

Preston chuckled a little. "No, I just mean," he began. "I think it's easier to talk to women about some things. Like, I've got my roommate, Brett, right? Been my best friend since freshman year, and it's like, there's just some... psychological thing blocking me from saying anything real to him, you know?"

Dalia paused for a second. "Preston, do you have anyone in your life that you can talk to? Really talk to?" Her voice was low, filled with a detectable sincerity and concern.

"Well there's you."

"Anyone *really* in your life, I mean."

"And you're *really* in my life."

"You know what I mean."

Preston swallowed hard and sort of licked his lips then bit his lower one in thought for a moment. "No, not really," he eventually answered.

"Family?"

"Not really. I mean, my family is... fine. I love them. We get along and everything, but it was never- I don't know, we were never really close in that sense, I guess."

"In what sense, then?"

"Well, they fed and housed me for eighteen years. They're paying for me to waste my time here. We were just never really a... you know, an emotionally open family. I haven't seen my family since the summer and they're like an hour away, tops."

"Have they talked to you at all about Ophelia?"

"Yeah, a little here and there. They were there for me, I can't really complain. I was just never really comfortable opening up to them, for some reason. My mom wanted me to go to... some doctor in Montpelier. I love my parents. And my brother's kind of an asshole, but I love him too. But I think my dad would go his whole life without talking to anyone if he could. Maybe that's where I got it from."

"I never knew my father really," Dalia suddenly said. Her statements about her own life were few

51

and far between, so at each one Preston latched onto every word. "He left when I was a toddler."

"Oh, really? That must have been tough," Preston uttered, since he didn't know what to say.

"I guess it was. At the time it didn't make a difference to me, I didn't remember him, really. Didn't know there was an alternative until I was in school and got to see all the other kids with two parents."

"What about your mother? Are you close with her?"

"She died eight years ago."

"Oh, sorry to hear that."

"Close is… a way to describe us," Dalia continued. "We fought a lot while I was growing up."

"What about?"

"Oh, everything. We were both… stubborn, I guess. She had a lot of boyfriends coming in and out of the picture, money was always an issue, she drank a lot, I drank a lot as soon as I got to high school, smoked too."

"Really?"

"Yeah, I was a bit of a handful. She didn't agree with what I wanted to do with my life, I didn't agree with what she was doing with hers. But, all we had was each other, so we always had to come around eventually."

"She didn't want you to be a writer?"

"Writing wasn't really my first career path, believe it or not."

"What was?"

Dalia paused, and even chuckled wistfully into the phone. "Music. I wanted to be a singer."

"Well, you can't just tell me that and not sing for me," Preston said.

Dalia laughed. "Well, that particular dream didn't happen for a reason, namely that I couldn't sing."

"Come on."

"Maybe one day."

"Today is one day."

"And there will be many more after today."

"So, it's gonna be like that, huh?"

"Absolutely it is," he could hear her smirking furtively through the phone.

"You have to promise me though."

"I promise."

"What do you promise?"

She sighed playfully. "You know."

"Words matter, Dalia," he teased.

"You know what? I should probably go to bed, I have to wake up early in the morning."

"Oh, come on, don't be like that."

"No, I really have to sleep."

"You don't *have* to sleep."

He heard her exhale sharply through her nose. "I, Dalia Peterson, do so swear that in the near future I shall sing for Preston Carter, so help me God. You can't see it, but I'm raising my right hand right now."

"Alright then."

A silence passed between them. Not an awkward pause but an intimacy that simply didn't require words. "So, what is it you want to do with your life, Preston?"

Preston sighed heavily into the phone. "Why do you ask?"

"Well, we've been talking all this time and I haven't even asked you the first question you ask a student: what's your major? I shared, now it's your turn."

"And I like talking to you because you didn't ask me shit like that," he laughed.

"Touchy subject?"

"Yeah, but we've already gone far past touchy, so fuck it. Truth be told... I got no clue. I switched my major three times this year."

"A little indecisive, are we?"

"Just a little. It's just... You know, it's hard to find something that doesn't seem completely miserable to devote your life to. Everyone says college is the best time of your life, but I just feel like I'm wasting it feeling sorry for myself and trying to decide what the hell to do. Sometimes I feel like I just... totally missed out on my youth."

"Because of Her?"

Preston paused. "In part, more recently. But She also gave me the best parts of my life, so I can't really... you know. I just mean in a more general sense, I guess. Like, after this I'm gonna get a job and then I'll just be... waiting around to die if I don't do all this shit right."

"I don't think you're missing out. I think that just is youth."

"I wish I could just make a fucking decision for once."

"It isn't set in stone, you know. I went to community college, majored in education."

"Education?"

"Can you believe it?"

They both laughed. "Is there a lot of overlap between education and erotica?"

"You laugh, but really I learned how to write from learning to teach English."

"And you used your powers for sin," he teased.

"Oh, stop it-" Dalia's giggle was suddenly cut off. Preston heard a noise he couldn't identify on her end of the line, a sort of thumping. And then silence.

"Hello?" Preston ventured. There was no response for a moment. "Dalia?" he asked, more urgently. He listened carefully and could hear the vague whisper of her voice through the phone. And then another voice. He had no hope of making out what they were saying, but they were definitely there. "Dalia, is everything good?"

A moment later, her voice was back in the foreground. "I need to go, Preston."

Before he could begin to formulate a response, she was gone, and once again he was left alone, empty.

7

Another twenty-four hours passed. It was a Saturday, and Preston didn't have any classes, so instead he spent most of the day in the apartment, either lounging around on the futon with a building illness rising from his stomach into his chest or pacing around the single room aimlessly. Brett watched him with curiosity and concern in equal measure, but only briefly attempted to intervene. "Are you okay, dude? Shouldn't you be studying for your finals?" he asked in one such attempt, sitting on the futon with a bag of tortilla chips while Preston paced.

"I'll be fine," Preston groaned in response. He had already attempted to study a few times, but his mind was racing too fast with possibilities.

"Are you sure, dude? I never studied for a final and look where it got me."

"Yeah, well you also didn't go to any of your classes, and you didn't even bother showing up for one of your finals."

"Hey, that's not true, I was there. I just don't remember being there. Or the day before. Or why I brought a cantaloupe." Brett looked up at the ceiling, his face twisted as he attempted to retrieve the memory. "I still got a C in that class," he shrugged and gave up. "C's get degrees."

"You don't have a degree," Preston growled. "And barring another Cantaloupe Incident, I think I'll be fine."

"Whatever you say, dude," Brett conceded. He munched on some more chips and let that be the only sound in the apartment for a brief interlude. "I feel like we haven't talked in a while," he suddenly said.

Preston stopped his pacing and stared at Brett. "Do you have something you want to talk about?"

Brett thought for a moment. "Do you?"

"Not particularly."

Once more Brett stopped to think. "How you doing?" he finally asked.

"I'm fine, man."

"Cool. Cool," he nodded.

The apartment was silent for the rest of the afternoon.

Night came. The apartment was still silent. Preston was still restless. He kept his phone in his palm always, waiting for a notification.

Preston always hated being the one to call or message first, it made him feel like he was imposing himself on the other person, but by the time their usual appointment came around with no call, he could no longer resist. After a few drafts, he typed out a message to Dalia: a simple "is now a good time?"

He pressed send.

And he immediately regretted it.

The waiting became all the more unbearable, now that she was actively not acknowledging him, and the eleven minutes before she replied felt like an eternity. "Not really" one message came in. "We can text if you want" another said.

"okay, that's fine" he answered.

He struggled to come up with a following text for about four minutes, and so was thankful when she sent him "How are you"

No question mark, he carefully noted. "i'm doing alright." he blatantly lied. "finals are next week, so that's a whole thing"

"You'll be fine" she reassured him after seven minutes.

He immediately started typing again. "i feel like i don't even care anymore, you know?" he paused before sending.

"I understand" she simply said after twelve minutes.

Two words. He started typing again. "i guess i just feel like i'm not invested in school at all cause i have no idea what i'm doing or where i'll end up." He sent the message and started typing again when she didn't respond in six minutes. "do you ever feel like you don't even know who you are?"

Another nineteen minutes. "No I was always pretty sure of myself, what I wanted to do" she eventually responded.

"are you sure you can talk? you seem busy"

Thirteen minutes. "I am" followed by "Sorry bit tied up in a whole thing. Probably for the next few days"

"i'll leave you alone then."

Five minutes. "You don't have to"

"no no, i'll let you get to it."

Nothing.

A familiar dread arose in his chest. He wasn't alone, but that didn't stop the loneliness. If anything, others were making it worse. The way that they were tolerating him. The way that they were pitying him. The way that, no matter how hard he tried, he could never make them feel what he felt, not really. Couldn't make them know him or care to.

He was too tired to sleep, so instead he got up and crept past the slumbering Brett to grab the bottle of vodka on top of the fridge and drag it back to his room by the neck.

8

Preston was in the middle of his final final exam of the semester, when he felt a vibrating in his pocket. His phone rattled against the steel frame of his chair, and a few heads shot up from their exams and looked in his direction. He sort of half-waved in awkward apology and lowered his head, burying himself further into his exam. But as he was trying to conjure up an essay on military, economic, and cultural cooperation and competition between the Dutch and the Japanese in the seventeenth and eighteenth century, all he could think about was the buzz. Wondering whether it was her. Even though he knew it wasn't, it couldn't be, she never contacted him this early, and besides, it had been days since they talked.

Still, he managed to cut through the fog of his mind enough to scrawl out his essay. In fact, he had tossed in his exam well before most of the class had finished. He scrabbled in his pocket for his phone as soon as he exited the classroom.

It was her.

A simple message: "Are you free to talk now?"

"yeah" he instantly typed out and sent.

He kept walking, and by the time he found himself outside, striding the campus, his phone began ringing again. He looked down, saw Ophelia's face, and accepted the call. "Hey," he said into the phone.

"Hello, Preston," Dalia's voice said. Preston pictured her standing in the kitchen of a lavish Los Angeles estate, fixing up lunch. Her auburn hair was still a little unkempt from having woken up. She was dressed in nothing but a silky rose colored robe, the phone wedged between the side of her face and her shoulder as she strode around.

"So, what's up?" he asked her in a friendly tone.

"Oh, I was just wondering how your finals went."

"Uh… Fine I think."

"What's wrong?"

"Nothing, nothing, I just- well, you don't usually call this early in the day."

"Well I had a free moment or two, and… well, I suppose I missed you," she said in such a way that Preston couldn't begin to determine if she was joking or not.

"I, uh… Gotta be honest, I didn't really expect you to call me again at all."

"Why's that?"

"Well, you know, we haven't really talked in a while… I don't know, I figured you got bored of me or I annoyed you or something."

"I kept texting you."

"Yeah, but it was all, like, three-word answers… I don't know, like you were just kind of

61

keeping a bare minimum out of pity or some-thing."

"I told you, Preston, you don't have to worry about that. If I keep up contact with you, it's be-cause I want to. And if I don't, you'll know. I'm not going to waste my time keeping up appear-ances. No consequences, remember?"

"Right, I guess that makes sense. It was no big deal, anyway," Preston said. It was.

Preston came to a bench, wiped some mushy brown snow off it, and fell down in its cradle. "Well, I'm sorry you felt that way anyway," Dalia said.

"So, what've you been up to?"

"Oh, a whole storm of shit. Family things, mostly. And my publishers have been giving me all kinds of grief."

"Are you writing again?"

"I am, actually. My writer's block broke, hard and fast. I wrote a novella in the last couple weeks, just got it back from the editors."

"Wow, that's great."

"The publishers don't want it. 'Too dark, too niche,' they said."

"Eh, fuck 'em."

"I agree, but I'm locked in a contract for a few more books with them, so I can't shop it around right now. I might just self-publish it."

"Well, you've got a good following, right?"

"I do."

"Can I read it?"

"When it comes out. I think you'll like it."

"What's it about?"

"I'll keep it a surprise for you."

Preston stretched out to lay down on the bench and put sunglasses over his face as he kept talking with her. He watched the sun arc down in the sky, bundled in his coat and a beanie. Passersby saw him with a wide grin on his face the entire time, and occasionally heard him break out in a chuckle. Sometimes he closed his eyes behind the tinted lenses and tried to picture her there, next to him. He made a decision lying there on that bench, just about the only decision he himself had made in a long time. When they finally ended the call, he looked on the screen and saw that it had lasted one hour thirty-seven minutes and forty-four seconds.

As he got up from the bench and began to walk back to his car, he scrolled through his contacts until he got the O's and stopped on Ophelia Lawson. He paused a moment before he changed the picture back to the default faceless silhouette, and slowly deleted each letter of Her name, and replaced it with a simple "Dalia."

Preston got in the Civic and drove home in silence, the radio shut off and his foot pressing firmer and firmer on the gas pedal.

When he burst through the door of their apartment, Brett was waiting for him, sitting at the kitchen counter. "How'd it go, dude?" he quickly greeted him.

Preston didn't respond for a moment. "Hey, Brett, you got an uncle out in Anaheim, right?"

Brett was confused to silence for a moment, but eventually responded, "Yeah, Uncle Quade."

"And is that the uncle who burned down your house?"

"Nah, that was Uncle Jeb."

"So, you're on good terms with Quinn?"

"Dude," Brett said, exasperated. "His name is Quade. I *just* said it."

"You know what I mean."

"I love Quade, man. He's like the father I only very briefly had. In a totally non-incestuous way."

"That's not- I didn't-" Preston sighed and moved on. "What do you say to a road trip?"

New York

1

Brett smiled from the passenger seat of the Civic, basking in the warmth of the heater, which only worked on his side. Preston tapped his fingers on the steering wheel and even began slapping the roof with his free hand along with the beat of "Never Going Back Again" by Fleetwood Mac rattling out of the car speakers. "This is good," Brett announced over the music. "This is a bonding experience." Preston simply sort of nodded along. "I think this is exactly what you need."

Again, Preston nodded his head. "Right on, man."

There was silence for a moment, if you can call the bumping frame and raspy speaker of the Civic a silence. Then Brett spoke up again, "So…" he began. "What's out in Anaheim for you?"

Preston shrugged. "Nothing in particular. We've always talked about heading out there like this."

Brett furrowed his brow. "No, we haven't."

"Yeah, man, a few times."

"I would've remembered that."

"You only remember, like, forty percent of the last three years, tops."

"Well, I might have forgotten stupid shit, like, 'What was I doing last night?', 'Where did I leave my keys?', 'Where did I leave my pants?', 'What's my roommate's name?'"

"You forgot my name?"

"But, I always remembered the important shit. Like when we talked about our dreams and stuff."

"Well, you forgot this one." Brett was evidently not convinced. "Look, I've never seen... the Pacific. Or anything west of, like, Detroit. Like you said, this is a goddamn, uh... What'd you call it?"

"Bonding experience?"

"Bonding experience, right, that's what it is. I don't have any, you know, ulterior motives here or anything."

Brett apparently accepted this, since he was quiet for more than a few moments, only the music of the car's speakers speaking. Mostly he just stared out the window at the long, straight, empty highway and snow coated forest before them beneath the afternoon sun. At one point, however, he turned around in his seat and looked at the contents of the car behind him. He and Preston each only needed one or two duffel bags to pack all the essentials they needed, and another smaller bag for other items likes books and laptops, and these were all thrown way back in the trunk. However, in the back seat were numerous cardboard boxes, one of which held what looked like pillows and blankets and the others all filled with food.

Brett's first order of business was to reach back and dive his hand into one of the boxes and eventually come up with a granola bar in hand. Next, as he was unwrapping and taking his first bite of the bar, he asked Preston, "So, do we know where we're staying tonight yet?"

Preston hesitated and didn't take his eyes off the road. "Well, man... I kinda figured, uh... Well you took that economics class once, right?"

"No."

"Oh," Preston began again. "Well, still, I thought that you might appreciate a little... fiscal responsibility. So I figured we could just... you know, sleep in the car. Or something like that, I don't know."

"Oh," Brett said. "That's, uh... That's interesting." A momentary pause. "Hey, Preston, did you bring, like, uh... money and shit?"

"Uh..."

"Because you know that I have like, 6.58 to my name, tops, right?"

"Well, I brought, uh, you know... I brought *some* money."

"Well, how much are we talking, dude?"

"I don't know, uh..." he waved a hand after a brief silence. "I don't know."

"Take a wild guess."

Preston shrugged. "Tank of gas or two," he mumbled.

"A tank of gas?" Brett repeated.

"Or two."

"Dude," Brett shouted. "The Civic is a fine vehicle, but we're gonna need more than a tank of gas-"

"Or two."

"Or two, to get across the country. And that's not even counting the fact that we need to eat.

And it's gonna be fucking freezing in this car at night."

"There's food back there, man. I brought blankets and shit."

"I don't really want to spend weeks eating granola bars and beef jerky and cold fucking canned beans."

"We can heat up the beans, man, I know how to build a fire."

"You're talking like a hobo, Preston, a hobo. You know who builds fires to heat up their canned beans? Hobos."

"First of all, I don't think 'hobo' is the... proper nomenclature."

"Dude-"

"I think 'homeless persons' would be-"

"Where are you gonna get wood? Did you bring a fucking axe?" Preston didn't respond. "How were you planning on getting the money we need to get the rest of the way to Anaheim? Because a tank of gas-"

"Or two."

"Is that counting the one we got back in Burlington?"

"Okay, one tank of gas."

"Jesus, dude."

Preston shrugged. "I don't know, I figured we could do... Odd jobs or something."

Preston felt his chest thumping as Brett was quiet. He didn't dare look over to the passenger's seat. "Odd jobs?" Brett asked quietly.

"Yeah, man, odd jobs."

"Odd jobs?" Brett shouted. "Who the fuck does odd jobs? This ain't fucking Middle Earth where we can just make a living adventuring and doing odd jobs."

"Well, we don't need a living, man, just like, a few more tanks of gas."

"How were you planning on finding odd fucking jobs?"

Again, Preston shrugged. "I don't know, maybe... Craigslist or something."

"Dude, the only thing that you're gonna find on Craigslist are dudes who want to murder you or sell you furniture or want you to jerk off onto their cat or something. And none of that pays."

"Well, look, man, we'll figure it out. Just- uh, just go with the flow, you know?"

"We should just turn around right now, head back."

"I'm gonna have to veto that," Preston shook his head. That wasn't an option, no matter how horribly ill-conceived this adventure was.

"Dude, we're gonna end up stranded in fucking Indiana or something at this rate."

"I hear Indiana is lovely this time of year."

"Indiana is never lovely, and you know it. Quaint at best."

"Come on, man, where's your adventurous spirit?"

"Oh, I think I left it at the apartment, let's go back and get it."

"If you want to be a successful, uh, business-man-"

"Entrepreneur, dude, there's a difference."

"Entrepreneur, okay. You gotta take, you know, risks. How do you think Zuckerberg and

Bill Gates made it, huh? By sitting on our couch in our apartment all day?"

"Well, I've never seen them there."

"Exactly, they just pushed forward. No matter the, uh, risks or whatever. And that's what you gotta do, with me, right now."

Brett shook his head and looked out at the road ahead. "This is the stupidest shit we've done in a while."

"But is it the stupidest thing we've done ever?"

Brett did not respond. And so, the car kept moving forward.

2

It was only an hour or so after their argument, the sun hanging just a notch lower in the sky, partly hidden behind thin, pale grey clouds. For the sake of making use of its GPS, Preston's phone was laying right on the dashboard, clearly in his line of sight. So, his eyes were instantly drawn to the notification that popped up on the top of his screen. He saw the name Dalia Peterson in it before it quickly disappeared again. He drove on for a few more moments, his eyes darting between the road and his phone, and eventually he turned to Brett. "You mind if I tag out now?" he asked.

"Alright," Brett responded.

Preston pulled the car over on the side of the highway and he and Brett awkwardly hurried out around the car and sat down in the opposite seats. As soon as he was a passenger, Preston reached for his phone off the dashboard and looked at the notification. There were two, in fact, both of them news alerts. On the first, Preston only saw the words "U.S.-Russian tensions continue to escalate as-" before he quickly swiped it away.

"News about Dalia Peterson" the second read. This one he opened. It led him to an article on a site that he had never heard of before, with a headline reading "Dalia Peterson Releases Surprise Novella Online." He kept reading, but the article didn't really provide much information besides a list of Dalia's previous works, her enigmatic nature, the fact that this novella had not been advertised at all before its release, and that it was currently only available in an eBook format, but physical copies might be on the way. There was a link at the bottom of the article to where you could find the book for sale.

Preston clicked the link.

The title of the book was emblazoned across his screen in a white, generic font within a blue speech bubble on a white background. "Sexting" and then in another speech bubble right beneath it "a novella by Dalia Peterson." At the bottom of the cover was a phone lying on its back with a thoroughly cracked screen. Instantly Preston pressed the purchase button, using five of the last eight dollars and forty-two cents in his checking account.

The book downloaded onto his phone, taking only a minute or so. He instantly opened it and began skimming through its contents. He stared at his phone for the rest of that day's ride, reading on as the sun sunk through the sky and Brett attempted in vain to start a conversation several times.

The book began with a vivid recounting of the daily life of a young woman, just out of college and into the adult world, living alone in a tiny studio apartment in San Francisco. Her name was Jessica. She didn't know anyone in the city, didn't know anyone really, so for the most part her phone was little more than a paperweight or something for her to idly browse through in a desperate attempt to distract herself from misery, drugs, and suicidal thoughts. But then one night, it rang.

She didn't recognize the number so she let it go to voicemail, and listened to the message the next morning.

It was Preston on the voicemail.

Not him literally, but it was his words, his confession, his pain.

The man on the voicemail would call her selfish, call her a bitch, but he would always end his messages with "I love you" or "I miss you." He was obviously drunk, maybe high on a few of the calls. Jessica decided to pick up the phone one night and finally get rid of the man.

She was Dalia, sometimes quoting her verbatim.

The next morning, the man apologized via text message with the same explanations Preston had. And Jessica used that same opening line: "You really shouldn't be harassing your ex like that."

The following conversations weaved in and out of fiction, at times near perfect transcripts of what Preston and Dalia had said to one another, at times totally fabricated, though even these felt so visceral, the emotions driving them so familiar that Preston questioned his own memory.

The details were changed, but the story essentially the same: the man was named Victor, and he was a student at UC Berkeley. His girlfriend had killed herself merely a month ago, and he had since attempted suicide himself.

Her name was still Ophelia.

The last portion of the book had not yet occurred, and it was strange for Preston to see put to paper essentially what he had been daydreaming of since he started this pilgrimage. One day, Jessica and Victor's relationship transcended the mere technological when he showed up on her doorstep. They didn't say a word to each other, he just kissed her.

In the middle of Preston reading a simultaneously beautifully poetic and disgustingly graphic description of their subsequent intercourse, he was brought back to reality by a small but noticeable thud, and then the Civic slowing down and swerving to the side of the road. Preston lifted his head from his screen and turned to Brett. "What's up, man?"

Brett's face was grim, and his voice cracked with sorrow. "I- I think I just hit a squirrel, dude."

"Oh, that sucks, man."

The Civic came to halt, pulled over on the side of the empty highway. Brett went rummaging through his pockets. "Why are we stopping?" Preston asked.

"I need to report this to the authorities, dude."

Preston paused for a moment as Brett fished out his phone. "Um…" Preston began. "You really don't."

"I will not leave that poor squirrel as roadkill for some vulture to swoop up."

"But that's just like… the cycle of life, man."

"I had a pet squirrel as a kid, dude."

"Of fucking course you did."

"His name was Gary."

"Of fucking course it was."

"I'm telling you, dude, squirrels aren't so different from us."

"I mean-" Preston was interrupted by the sound of Brett's phone ringing, on speaker. Preston looked over at his screen and saw that he was calling 911. "Jesus, Brett."

Brett shushed him as the operator picked up the phone. "Hello, 911, what's your emergency?"

"Hi, yeah, umm..." Brett gulped hard, choking back tears. "I just- I hit a squirrel, on the highway."

"Okay..."

"So, can you, like, send someone out here or something?"

"Um... That's it?"

"Yeah."

"Well... No."

Brett paused. "But, why?"

"We can't- It's just a squirrel."

"It was a living being, dude, don't disrespect it like that."

"Look, we can't just send a guy for every squirrel, you know?"

"That's not cool, dude. Not cool at all. What am I supposed to do?"

"Just kinda... keep driving?"

"Not cool. I'm not just gonna leave this little guy behind."

"Brett, just let it go-" Preston interrupted.

"No, this is about the sanctity of life, dude. What the hell am I supposed to do with this... this formerly living being, that probably had a family and emotions and shit?"

"Well..." the operator began. "Do you want it?"

"Do I want it?"

"Yeah. Squirrel meat isn't so bad, bro. Don't knock it till you try it."

"I'm not gonna eat it, this squirrel is my friend."

"I'm serious, bro. This one time I was camping with my dad, in the Finger Lakes, and I forgot to pack the cooler, and he was like 'Kevin, you fucking idiot, you forgot the cooler.' I'm Kevin, by the way. Then he kinda... beat me with a branch for a while, but that night he killed a squirrel and made me eat it, and it was-"

The voice was abruptly cut off as Brett hung up the phone with a fury. "Fuck, dude," he sighed, more to himself than Preston. "Emergency services can't help us."

"Not with squirrels."

"Our institutions are crumbling, dude. Crumbling."

Brett looked around the back seat of the car, and eventually grabbed one of the boxes filled with food and dumped an assortment of granola bars and chips and beef jerky all over the back seat.

"What are you doing?" Preston asked.

"Follow me, dude."

Brett pushed open his car door and took the cardboard box with him as he exited out onto the highway. "It's fucking cold out there," Preston shouted before unclicking his own seatbelt and following, mumbling to himself as he did. "Sanctity of fucking life."

Brett was walking down the middle of the lane, in the direction that would be against traffic if the road wasn't desolate and depopulated. The Civic was still running behind him, the headlights providing a backlight to his march. He came to a halt a small distance from the car, where Preston caught up to him. It was indeed fucking cold out there. Preston looked down and instantly averted his eyes as he felt his stomach churn. "Jesus Tapdancing Christ," he groaned.

The squirrel lay at Brett's feet, bloodied and crumpled, a bit of gore strewn on the blacktop. "I'm sorry, buddy," Brett whispered sincerely. He turned to Preston. "Help me scoop him up, dude."

"I'm not gonna help you scoop him up, this was your fucking idea."

"Come on, dude. Help me scoop him."

"No, Brett. This is fucking absurd, man."

"This was a living being, dude. And I killed it. Don't you care about that?"

"Not particularly, at the moment."

"We're going to give it a proper burial. Help me scoop, goddammit."

"I am not gonna scoop. Brett, the squirrel is fucking dead. It's not like it's family is religious or something," Preston was raising his voice, it echoed out in the open highway surrounded by forest on either side. "It doesn't care. That's just, like, nature, man."

"This little fella deserves some dignity in his resting, and I'm not gonna let him freeze on the asphalt." Brett knelt down, and Preston kept his eyes on the forest, his back turned to the scene of the murder. He could still hear the cardboard scraping on the asphalt and the thud the squirrel made as it sank to the bottom of the box, followed by a few lighter thuds. He thought he was gonna throw up. "Come on, dude, it's done. We're gonna put him in the woods, where he belongs."

Before Preston could turn around and protest, Brett was already venturing into the wild. Preston sighed once more as he gave chase, following Brett's footsteps as he traced a path through the trees, holding the box gingerly in his hands with what could only be described as reverence. It became harder and harder for Preston to see Brett as they plunged into the forest, the trees blocking out all but a few luminescent strands of silvery moonlight shining on the snow that crunched beneath their feet. He nearly ran into Brett when he came to a halt in a small clearing. Brett knelt down to begin pushing aside snow and digging at the earth with his bare hands. Preston refused to help him, looking down at him as he clawed at the dirt.

Eventually, Brett seemed satisfied, despite the fact that he barely made a dent in the frozen earth, and picked up the box once more to dump its contents in the impromptu grave. A few bits and pieces came out before the body of squirrel itself rained into the hole, prompting a quiet, "Fuck," from Preston.

Brett rose to stand beside Preston and stare down at the corpse. "Would you like to say a few words, dude?"

"I'm good," Preston sighed one last time.

Brett paused before beginning his own speech. "I'm sorry I killed you, little dude," he announced in the most orotund baritone he could muster. "I love animals, and I didn't mean to cause you any harm. My only hope is that you didn't feel much pain or fear, and that you're at peace now," his voice broke at the end.

Silence ruled the forest for a moment, then Brett began kicking the small mound of dirt beside the hole back in, slowly masking the corpse in an earthen veil. *"Amazing grace,"* he began singing as he buried the squirrel. *"How sweet the sound."*

Preston chose to turn around and begin trudging back to the car instead of listening to Brett mumbling gibberish lyrics to a slightly altered version of the hymn's tune.

3

Later that night, the blood of the squirrel still freshly painted on the front left wheel of the Civic, Preston pulled the car into the nearly empty lot of a rest stop. Brett unbuckled his seatbelt. His face was still solemn as he asked Preston, "Do you want me to get you a snack or anything while I'm in there?"

"I'm good," Preston mumbled.

"Okay," Brett replied. "I think I'm gonna bathe myself in the sink in there, and that's probably gonna be a whole thing, so I might take a while."

"Do what you gotta do, man. I think we can sleep here, anyway."

"Alright, dude."

As soon as Brett left the car, Preston pulled out his phone. He had missed a call from Dalia. It was two in the morning, but he figured that they had had talks later, and besides she was on West Coast time.

The phone rang a few times before Dalia's voice appeared. "Preston," she said cheerfully.

"Hi Dalia," Preston said after a brief pause.

He got out of the car and paced around it while Dalia said, "Is something wrong?"

"Why do you ask?"

"I don't know, you seem... off," Dalia's voice had become just as soft as his.

"I've said six words."

"Still..."

"Eh, long day. Hey, I, uh... I saw that you put out that book."

"Oh, did you? It's getting a lot of buzz so far."

"I bet... Hey, you didn't tell me..."

"That I was writing a book about us?"

"Yeah, that."

"Well, what can I say, you inspired me." He could hear the grin in her voice. "You're my muse."

"Thanks..." Preston mumbled.

Dalia paused. "Seriously, what's wrong?"

Preston didn't answer for a minute. He stopped ambling and instead took a seat on the hood of the Civic. "Is..." He huffed, unable to find the words. "Is that all this was?"

"What do you mean?"

"I mean, am I just... some character to you?"

"Are you really giving me the 'What are we?' speech?"

"Yeah, to be perfectly honest," Preston took an edge of anger in his voice. "I... thought that this was something real, and now I'm just finding out it was all... research?"

"I never said that."

"Yeah, well…"

"You're being-"

"I care about you, Dalia. And I thought that you cared about me."

"I do care about you, Preston. Why would I still be talking to you if I didn't, the fucking book is out."

"But how do I know you weren't just using me?"

"I wasn't," she firmly said. "I think that we have a great story and I wanted to share it, that's all. I wanted to express what I'm feeling, the book was just gonna be for me, but then when I finished I realized it's the best thing that I've ever written. It's the kind of book that can really help people, Preston."

"So… what? That makes you Jessica?"

She paused. "In a way, yeah."

"You're alone like her?"

"Well, I was. Until I met you."

Preston laid down, his back against the windshield and his face staring up at the starry night. It was cold out, but he didn't particularly care. "Hey, how'd you know I was black, by the way? Everyone's always told me I talk white."

"What?"

"Victor, he's black, like me. How'd you know?"

"I, uh… To be perfectly honest, I didn't."

Preston laughed. "Oh, so is that like a cuckolding thing or something?"

"Look, I'm just writing what sells." They both laughed. "I honestly pictured you completely different."

"Well, I don't really look like Victor, to be honest. How'd you picture me?"

"I thought you were kind of lumberjackish. I guess because you're from Vermont."

"Well, my dad does grow Christmas trees on the farm, actually. But I don't look like a lumberjack. I don't think I've seen any other black lumberjacks, come to think of it."

"Do you have a beard?"

"Yeah, yeah I do."

"I knew it," she sounded genuinely excited. "What's your hair like?"

"Dreads."

"Really?"

"Yeah, but not like, big huge dreads. Like, *To Pimp a Butterfly* era Kendrick Lamar type dreads."

"Huh…"

"Didn't picture that?"

"Again, Vermont and all… Are you tall?"

"I am six foot four, and you can't prove otherwise." Again, they laughed together. "What about you? Do you look like Jessica?"

"Hm… Not really. We're both brunettes. My hair's longer though, just past my shoulders. She's a bit younger than me too."

"Do you have blue eyes?"

"Grey."

"Oh, even better."

"Thank you, thank you." There was a brief moment of silence.

"I wish I could see you," Preston said. "I… I wish I could just reach out and touch you."

She hesitated a bit. "Is that so?"

"Yeah."

"What would you do if you could?" she nearly whispered.

Preston felt his heart pounding into his ribcage. "You already wrote it."

"I know. But, I want to hear you say it."

Indiana

1

The Civic was sputtering, coughing and hacking in agony, dying on the road. It was traveling through the narrow city streets of Indianapolis, in the inner city. Rickety houses lined the streets, the windows emitting faint, warm light in the midst of the night that the Civic navigated. It was bitterly cold, but snow hadn't fallen yet.

Brett was behind the wheel of the Civic as it stopped accelerating and began to simply coast along the road, slowly losing its momentum. "I fucking told you, man," Preston said from the passenger seat. "We should've stopped at that gas station back there."

"It was only like a mile back, dude, we can walk," Brett said as he pulled the Civic over to the side of the road and it slowly came to a halt.

"We wouldn't have to walk if you just stopped."

"We need to make every drop of gas count, dude," Brett replied. "I'm not filling this bitch until she's empty."

"That's not how cars work."

"Well, irregardless, dude," Brett began as he took the key out of the Civic and unbuckled his seatbelt. "Unless, you wanna sleep here, we need to get some gas."

"Alright, have fun."

Brett was about to get out of the car, but instead turned his head in shock. He uttered a betrayed, "Dude."

"I'm not going. It was your decision that brought us here. Besides, this... doesn't look like a great neighborhood."

"I'm sure it's not that bad."

"Well, I'm not saying it's fucking Damascus or anything but-"

"Damascus is a city with a rich history and cultural heritage, dude. I'm sure this neighborhood is rich too. Rich in... character."

"Well, let me know if you're still so sure when you get stabbed."

"What's the worst that could happen?"

"Uh, we die."

"Everybody's gotta die someday, dude. Besides, we'll be safer if we have a buddy system." Preston sighed heavily before finally unbuckling his seatbelt and opening his door. Brett met him out on the streets after locking the car doors and said, "Thanks, dude, I appreciate it."

Preston didn't respond, just walked along and began their nighttime stroll, stuffing his hands deep in his pockets to avoid the chill. Things seemed quiet and peaceful enough, but every distant barking dog and every faded honking of a car horn made Preston whip his head.

About ten minutes of this passed when suddenly Brett spoke up. "Hey, Preston," he said in a soft, hesitant voice.

"What's up?"

"Well…" He began. "As you know, we're going to be passing through Kansas City on the way to Anaheim, and as you know, I was born and raised in the big KC-"

"What I know is that no one else in the fucking world calls it 'the big KC.'"

"Can you not interrupt me, dude? That was very rude."

"I'm sorry, go on," Preston resigned.

"And that is definitely a thing." Brett inhaled and began his pitch again, "As you may or may not know, the big KC is a land of amazing majesty and opportunity."

"Sure."

"There's a wonderful, amazing place there called Adventure Fun World and Water Fun World."

"Okay."

"It's an amusement park. But it is so much more than that. We went there all the time when I was a kid. And when I was a teenager. And every time I've come back since. So, I guess what I'm saying is that we should make a point to stop there."

"Yeah, sure man, whatever," Preston said, looking over his shoulder at the sound of a loud banging far away.

"Really?"

"Yeah."

"I'm holding you to that."

"Fine."

"Oh man," Brett chuckled. "You are going to fucking love it, dude. They got-"

The two were coming up to an alleyway between an apartment building and a Papa John's establishment. A man with a black hoodie and a pale face stepped out of the alley. Preston scanned the figure and didn't think too much of him until he came to a halt just before them and lifted a trembling hand, displaying a gun. "Gimme your fucking money," the man demanded in a soft tone, his breath visible in the cold.

"Woah, dude, not cool," Brett responded.

"Yeah, what the hell, man?" Preston said, more mildly perturbed than anything.

"Gimme your fucking money before I shoot your ass," the man repeated, slightly louder but stumbling over his words.

"Seriously, dick move, man," Preston moaned.

The gun clicked as the man turned it on Brett. "Empty out your pockets."

"I'm wearing cargo pants, dude, that's gonna take forever."

"I got all fucking night."

Brett sighed and began rifling through each of his pockets. "What do you even need this money for?"

"I'm gonna buy some crack rock."

"Dude, not kosher. I don't mean to be judgmental or anything, but that is not a healthy lifestyle. I wouldn't even be bothered if you said you were gonna feed your family or something."

"I'm not a liar," the robber sniffled.

Brett pulled out a half-eaten pack of Skittles from one of his pockets. "You had Skittles this whole time?" Preston asked.

"I'm sorry, dude, you know I'm bad at sharing sometimes."

"Gimme the skittles," the robber demanded. Brett sighed before reluctantly handing the packet over.

He pulled his earbuds and his phone out of one pocket and his wallet out of another, which was empty aside from an ATM card, his driver's license, several fake licenses, and a Chuck E. Cheese Play Pass, along with a few strands of prize tickets. "You're a twenty-two-year-old man," Preston shook his head, "why do you still have fake I.D.s?"

"Never know when you need to go undercover, dude."

"Brett-"

"Brett? Or… Hugh Babadopoulos?" Brett grinned and displayed one of the licenses.

"That just sounds like an appetizer at a Greek restaurant or-"

"Alright, that's enough of that," the robber said, turning the gun towards Preston. "Now you, with the nappy hair, turn out your pockets. And, uh… And don't, uh… Don't try to be a *gyro*."

"Woah, dude," Brett interjected.

"You know, like the, uh, like the sandwich?" the robber stammered. "It's Greek, so uh…"

"Is it pronounced like that?" Preston said. "I did not get that, man. I've just been saying jy-ros. All my life. Huh."

"I got the joke, and it was commendable, dude, but uh…" Brett was silent for a moment, shifting his gaze expectantly between the robber and Preston. "Can white people say 'nappy?'" he finally asked Preston.

"I mean, he's already robbing us, so..."

"Well, this man is a crack addict. He has an illness. That doesn't, you know, justify armed robbery, but at least there's a reason. There's no reason for casual racism, and I will not abide it."

"I wasn't really offended, to be honest. I mean, he was just trying to identify me."

"I- I didn't just want to say, 'Hey, you, black guy,'" the robber offered up. "That seemed a little, I don't know, aggressive, I guess."

"There's only two of us," Brett argued. "You didn't really have to say anything. Dude, I've been avoiding the word 'nappy' ever since I met this man, and now you're just walking up, calling him nappy."

"How often would you have an opportunity to say 'nappy?'" Preston asked.

"Is it, like, a *bad* word?" the robber asked. "I don't think it's necessarily like an *insult*. It's just... an adjective."

"I don't know. It just feels, like, ugh, you know?" Brett answered. "Like, I feel like I'm not supposed to say it, and when you said it, I was just kinda like 'Oooh, I don't know how I feel about that.'"

"I think it *can be* kinda... loaded, you know?" Preston said. "But I guess it depends on the context."

"I'm half Hispanic, by the way, if that, uh... if that makes a difference," the robber interjected.

"Really?" Preston said. "You're pale as hell, no offense."

"Well, my dad's Irish, so you know, it kinda cancels out. Plus, there's the whole… crack thing."

"Oh really? You know I can see it, now," Preston said, Brett nodding in agreement.

"Yeah, dad's like a fucking leprechaun, it's ridiculous."

"Oh," Brett said, "is he a, um… a little… person?"

"No, no, he's five foot nine, I just meant, you know, more in the… hair and beard and face department."

"So, what's your name?" Preston asked.

"It's, uh, Alejandro O'Donnelly." They all laughed together for a moment, the robber still raising his gun. "Yeah, so you can see-" suddenly he stopped and rubbed his face with his unarmed hand. "Aw shit, I shouldn't have said that, now you can report me to the police. Fuck, dude." Alejandro sighed heavily. "Okay, um… That's, uh- That wasn't- That was a joke, that's not my real name, got it?"

"Well anyway, being a, uh… racial minority doesn't… preclude you from being prejudiced yourself, dude."

"Well, Brett, tell you what," Preston said. "This man has been very kind, so I say we give him the benefit of the doubt."

Brett paused. "Alright, alright."

"Yeah, I really didn't mean to come off like that," Alejandro shrugged.

"Well," Preston began, "now you know, it's, uh- it's kind of a grey area and, you know, I think we all learned a little something from this experience. Very... productive." The two nodded in agreement. "Cool. Now, uh... good day, sir," Preston said, beginning to turn.

"Hold up, hold up," Alejandro said, keeping the gun raised at Preston. "Nuh uh, you're not gonna bamboozle me, kid. You didn't give me your shit yet."

Preston grimaced. "Man, this is my last couple bucks, we gotta get to L.A.-"

"Anaheim," Brett corrected.

"Anaheim, yeah, right. We're completely out of gas-"

"And I'm completely out of crack."

Preston sighed. "Fine, fine."

He took out his wallet and took the last tank of gas money that was left in there and handed it over to Alejandro. Alejandro counted it out for a moment, then looked back up at the two. "Pleasure doing business with you," he said. Then he instantly shot into a full sprint the other way down the road.

"Wow," Brett said, watching the sprint. "Look at him go. He doesn't look like he'd be that fast. Cool guy, though."

"Shut the fuck up, Brett." Preston rubbed his brow. "We're broke, now. Shit. I've got, like, three bucks on my debit card. That'll get us... a gallon or so... We're fucked."

Brett stared off at the horizon into which Alejandro had disappeared for another moment. "Come on, dude," he eventually said. "Let's go."

Brett went striding off, continuing on their route to the gas station. "Go where?" Preston called out to him, not yet following.

Brett simply marched on, giving him no answer. Preston called out after him as he broke into a light jog to catch up with him.

2

"Brett," Preston called out to the figure striding forward a few steps ahead of him, silhouetted against the lights of a gas station parking lot. "Where the hell are you going? We don't have any money."

"Just follow me, dude," Brett said as he entered the aura of light around the gas station and its attached convenience store.

Brett advanced further, straight through the glass door and the bell that rang as it swung open. Preston finally caught up with him at the back of the store, next to the bathrooms out of which had just stepped a rather portly old man whom Preston had to squeeze by in order to get to Brett. Brett's face was awash with the glow of a screen as he looked down at an ATM and inserted a card. "You had money in the bank this whole fucking time?"

"I do."

"How much are we talking about?"

Brett paused. "Two thousand one hundred fourteen dollars and sixty-four cents."

"Jesus fucking Christ..." Preston scoffed. "Why didn't you say anything?"

Brett sighed, standing still and staring into the ATM's screen. "My mother gave me this money under the condition that I would only use it in the case of an emergency."

"Fine, fine, all that matters is that we got it now." Preston watched expectantly as Brett leaned over the screen, staring into the dull blue light. Brett was completely motionless for a moment. "What are you doing?" Preston asked.

Brett exhaled heavily through his nose. "Frankly, I'm not sure that this qualifies as an emergency, dude."

Preston stared at Brett. "You're fucking joking, right?"

"I would never joke about such a serious matter, Preston."

Preston sighed. "You know what's a serious matter, Brett? The fact that we are stranded in goddamn Indianapolis, with no goddamn money and no goddamn gas because we got robbed at gunpoint. How is that not a fucking emergency?"

"You raise a valid point," Brett conceded. "But we got ourselves in this situation, we chose to drive to Indianapolis. Maybe we should feel some of the consequences of that action, dude."

"I'm feeling it, man. I don't know about you, but I'm feeling the consequences hard."

"What I mean is that we should be getting ourselves out of this."

"Yeah, well, we have the means to right now, just withdraw the money."

"Dude, if I so much as sniff in the direction of that money, my mother is going to literally climb up my ass and murder me."

"Brett-"

"Up. My. Ass, dude."

"Your mom isn't here, and I'm sure she'll understand."

"We're supposed to stop in the big KC, dude. Not to mention, she'll just freeze the account soon as I touch it."

"I'm going to assume you mean Kansas City, but I refuse to acknowledge that as a legitimate name for it."

"I'm serious, dude, how am I supposed to look my mom in her good eye."

"You don't have to, man. We won't stop at your mom's place, we'll just stop at, uh... You know, Seas of Fun-"

"Adventure Fun World and Water Fun World, dude."

"Adventure Fun World and Water Fun World, right, think about that, huh. How are we gonna get to go there if we don't have money?" This line of argument Brett was unable to refute. He merely stood silently, still hunched over the ATM. "Look, I wasn't gonna say anything, you know, to keep up morale, but I've been thinking for a while, this whole trip was a bit fucking ill conceived, right? This is what we need, man. Just withdraw some now, we'll hit up a bank and get the rest of it tomorrow, so she can't freeze it on us. We'll put it back after, maybe we'll make some more money along the way and your mom won't even notice we took it."

Brett paused. "Mother, forgive me," he said softly as he pushed a few buttons, and a steady flow of cash erupted from the machine's maw.

He hastily stuffed the fresh bills in his pockets and turned away from the machine. Preston followed and patted him on the back. "You did good."

"I don't want to hear it, dude. I'm not proud of what we've done here." Brett stopped suddenly in the store's candy aisle, so much so that Preston nearly ran into him. "This changes nothing, dude," he said grimly. "This is for bare necessities only. We aren't spending a fucking cent we don't need to."

"Right on, no quality of life improvements."

"I'm serious."

Missouri

1

"Here you go, honey," the waitress said as she laid a plate down on the table. She was older woman, with the slight twang of a Missouri accent through the filter of a pack of cigarettes a day for twenty-three years in her voice. The plate she set down was more of a platter, with what would normally be a large stack of waffles dwarfed by every hash brown the small diner had readily available.

Brett, sitting down on the receiving end of the meal tipped his obviously brand new, yet somehow already mysteriously stained, Cardinals baseball cap. "Thank you kindly," he said with a smile.

"Hey," Preston intervened from across the table, already digging into his own stack of waffles, or more precisely one of his three. "Can I get a scotch and soda?"

"We lost our liquor license back in '03," the waitress said.

"Alright," Preston failed to hide his disappointment. "Just water then?" he said with a smile.

The waitress returned a halfhearted smile which instantly dissipated as soon as she turned around. Preston's eyes wandered up to a fat, senile television in the corner, turned to the news. The left side of the screen was mostly taken up by shots of a small panel of people yelling. Their voices were muted and the subtitles turned off, but somehow Preston knew what they were saying. The right half was switching between a still image of a black child and a video of the streets of several cities crowded with people, some holding signs scrawled with slogans and the name "Lavar Gray," some breaking windows and breaking out into fights. Beneath it all was the headline "PRO-TESTS OVER VERDICT IN POLICE SHOOTING CASE." Preston tried to keep his eyes away and focused on Brett as he reached into one of the pockets of his cargo pants and pulled out a small bottle of hot sauce and applied it liberally to the entirety of his plate.

"That's disgusting," Preston said. "Hash browns, fine, I can accept that. But waffles? Syrup, whipped cream, maybe some fruity shit if you're feeling fancy, those are the only acceptable toppings."

"This is my right as a human being and an American citizen, we've been over-" Brett suddenly cut off his speech when stray droplets of hot sauce appeared on his stomach. "Ah fuck, dude," he said, loud enough to prompt a series of looks from all around the diner.

Preston hastily grimaced and waved in apology to the spectators. "Calm down, man," he growled in a low voice.

"I just got this shirt, look at it," Brett said. He held out the front of his shirt to display the crimson stains, dashed over the word "reached," in the phrase "I reached the top of the St. Louis Gateway Arch and all I got was this stupid t-shirt," that was scrawled in a navy blue, sickeningly fun font across the white shirt, wrapping around a picture of the Arch.

"You shouldn't've gotten that shirt anyway," Preston said, looking down at his own freshly purchased red hoodie with the words "Property of St. Louis, Missouri" in an arch on his chest. "It's…" his voice trailed off.

"Finish what you were gonna say," Brett demanded.

"No."

"Do it."

"I don't want to."

"You were gonna say it's stupid," he grinned.

Preston merely sighed.

"See, that's why it's so good, dude, it's self-referential. And look who's talking… generic hoodie wearing ass."

"Now that's just uncalled for."

"It's perfectly called for, dude," Brett said through a mouth full of hash browns. As Brett was mashing the hash browns in his maw, he watched Preston flinging his eyes around the diner between bites of his waffles. "What's the matter, dude?"

"Huh?" Preston snapped his gaze back to Brett.

"You're jumpy, why are you jumpy?"

"I'm not jumpy."

"You're jumpy," Brett insisted.

Preston paused and once more scanned their surroundings. "I don't know… Just, you know."

He lowered his voice. "We're kinda in the sticks here. Makes me nervous, is all."

"Alright, Vermont boy."

"You know what I mean. My dad always warned me about going to… places like this that I didn't know."

This time it was Brett letting his eyes look around the diner. "That guy over there looks… ethnic." Preston began to turn in his seat. "Don't look at him, dude," Brett hissed.

"Well, what's he look like?"

"I wanna say… Filipino?"

Preston's phone was lying on the table besides his feast, and suddenly sprung to life, lighting up and vibrating against the table. Instantly, Preston dropped his utensils, disregarded his meal and picked up the phone. Dalia's name was there in the light, an incoming call. "I gotta take this," he barely managed to utter through a mouthful of waffle as he shot up from the table and moved towards the door.

"Where you going, dude?" Brett called back to no response as he watched Preston walk out of the diner and stop on the sidewalk, the phone already to his ear.

"Hey there," Preston said into the receiver. He realized that he had left his bomber jacket back in the booth and now he was shivering on the sidewalk.

"I want you to fuck me, Preston," Dalia's voice appeared at the other end of the line.

"What now?" Preston said as he watched a family of four pass him, entering the diner.

"I want you to fuck me."

Preston paused. "What? Now?"

"Tell me what you would do to me again."

Preston whirled his head around, examining his surrounding and finding people everywhere. "I'm, uh… I'm kinda in public right now," he said in a low tone.

"Oh, you're shy now?"

Preston looked out at the parking lot and saw a man approaching on foot, a black guy, middle aged, dressed in an ill-fitting all white suit with a stack of papers in his hand. He didn't seem bothered by the cold, despite the fact that he didn't have a real coat or any other winter attire. He seemed to be walking directly towards Preston, even staring at him, but he was still some distance away so Preston did his best to ignore his advance. "A little bit," he said into the phone.

"Alright," Dalia whispered. "I'll do the talking then." The man in the white suit was getting closer and closer, not straying from his path towards Preston. "Do you remember the second to last chapter of the book?" Dalia spoke into Preston's ear.

"Yeah, I do," Preston responded. The man in the white suit was clearly looking at Preston now, and nodded to him. Preston returned the nod as the man continued to approach and took a piece of paper out of the stacks in his arm.

"Do you remember what Victor did with his tongue?" Dalia asked.

The man was now standing before Preston. He flashed a smile and thrust out the piece of paper. Preston took it, and by the time he had processed what had happened, the man was already moving

105

on, entering the diner. "Vividly," Preston responded to the phone.

Preston looked down at the piece of paper, a flyer. It was dominated by a question, written in white, shining font on a dark background: "Where will you go?" Below that, in what would have been gold text on a sky-blue background had the flyer been printed in color, the word "Heaven," and further below that, separated by an "or" was "HELL," nearly illegible in a swirl of various greys in the vague shape of a flame. At the very bottom of the flyer was an address, followed by "Pastor Jefferson Freeman, sermons every Sunday morning at 10! Free brunch foods!"

Preston was staring at the flyer, only broken out of the momentary trance by Dalia's voice in his ear once more. "Wouldn't you like to do that to me?"

"Uh… yeah, yeah, definitely." Preston whipped his head around back towards the diner, attempting to track the man in the white suit. He was handing out flyers and a smile to each table. "For sure."

"Is everything alright, Preston?" Dalia asked, suddenly returning to her natural voice.

The man reached the table where Brett sat alone with their food, and he placed a flyer down between Preston's stack of waffles and the shrinking sea of hash browns on the table. "Huh?" Preston said.

"I asked if everything was alright."

Preston watched as Brett called out to the man, and he turned around with yet another beaming smile. They began talking. "Yeah, yeah, I'm good, just a little distracted."

"Are you at your parents' place?" she asked.

"Nah, no, I'm uh… I'm still in Burlington." Preston watched as the man in white sat down where he had been, across from Brett, maintaining that full, luminescent smile.

"I thought that you said you were going back the week after finals?"

Preston had, of course, completely forgotten that he was meant to do just that. At least that explained why his mother had been calling him so much. He had been rejecting all her calls, resolving that dealing with his family would be a problem for Future Preston. "Uh, yeah, yeah, that was the plan, but, you know… that kinda fell through. As plans do."

"Well you should go see them soon, anyway."

"Yeah, right, definitely."

There was a momentary pause. "Seriously, Preston," Dalia voice grew grimmer. "Is everything alright? With us, I mean."

"Yeah, seriously, it's great. Why do you ask?"

"Well, the whole book thing, and the fact that we haven't talked in a while."

"I was just… I figured I'd let you call me this time."

"Really?"

"Yeah, I mean, I wanted to talk to you but I didn't want to… impose."

"Well, let's make this easier on everyone. If you want to talk to me, call me. And if I want to talk to you, I'll call you. And that's it. Deal?"

"Deal," Preston smiled.

"Tell you what, I need to go, and you're in public, so let's make an appointment for tomorrow night. I'll call you."

"Looking forward to it," Preston grinned.

"Me too." She hung up the phone.

Preston looked up, back to the diner, and saw that his booth was empty once more, the man in white disappeared.

2

"Now, for today's sermon, I'd like to talk with y'all about something that has been... clouding my mind these last few days." The pastor's deep, rich voice dribbled out of his mouth, flowing over the rows of pews before him as he paced around the front of the small, stuffy church, still dressed in his all white suit. "Well, truth be told, it's something that has troubled me just about as long as I could think, but only just recently have I been able to... wrap my mind around this aspect of our Lord Almighty," he twisted a hand in the air, as if illustrating the wrapping.

Preston and Brett sat alone in the very back row, behind several elderly couples. Preston was slouching in his seat and tapping his fingers against his thighs, his eyes scanning the room for anything that might alleviate the all-powerful boredom that swept over him. He had already skimmed the hymn book in front of his seat several times. Brett was next to him, sitting upright and pretending to be interested in the sermon for the sake of manners. Preston leaned over to him. "Why'd you make us come here?" he whispered.

"I'm gonna be honest with you, dude," Brett whispered in reply without taking his eyes off the pastor. "I thought this was gonna be one of the fun, black churches with the singing and all that."

"Fucking idiot," Preston grumbled.

An old woman from one of the couples ahead shot him a death glance and turned back around before he could react. "Look, dude, let's just stick it out for the free brunch," Brett said.

"I don't like churches, man," Preston grumbled.

"What, you gonna burst into flames or something?"

"They gotta smell to 'em."

He had never really noticed the overbearing must of a church hall back when his parents had briefly forced him to make the regular Sunday morning trips with them. He vividly remembered that he had first noted it at the funeral, when he was trying to think about anything other than the fact that She didn't exist anymore, not really, but She was still lying there, beneath the casket. He spent a long time studying the hall, the fabric of his black tie, the grain of the wooden pews, the way sweat was beading all over his body in the summer's blaze. The smell and the heat became suffocating. It was so goddamn hot. And then he spent another long moment just sitting outside, studying every blade of grass and every cloud. But he couldn't escape the heat.

The pastor continued. "As... men and women, human beings, mortals... We are all sinners. I don't care who you are, I don't care what color your skin is, where you're from, who you love, whether or not you follow our God, we are all sinners. You are a sinner," he began shouting and pointing at random members of the audience. Preston sunk a little lower in his seat. "You are a sinner. You are a sinner. You are a sinner. I am a sinner!

"Our mere existence is a sin, from the original sin onwards. And unless you are the Lord Jesus Christ Himself returned to this world, then none among us can claim to have lived completely innocent, godly lives." The pastor sunk a little, lowering his shoulders and his voice, turning his eyes towards the floor at a just noticeable angle. "Let me tell you, folks, I have been to the darkness. To the darkest places you can imagine. As most of y'all know by now, in my younger days I was an addict. I gambled. I drank. I shot up heroin. I lied, I cheated, I stole, I sold my body to women and men alike, anything that it took to get that next hit. There were times where I almost took my own life and ended this great gift that God has given us.

"And in those days, when I was told that God loved me, I thought only 'How? How can He love someone so wicked? Someone who has broken His laws a hundred times over? How can He love me when even I hate myself?' And even today, living in the light, I wonder, how can God create us as such tortured, flawed souls if He truly loves us? And how can He who is so perfect love us, the wicked and depraved? You need only to turn on the news to see the depths to which the human soul will sink… To see young boys gunned down in the streets… To see rioters tearing their own homes apart... And yet He still professes that He loves us."

The pastor paused and pulled a pair of reading glasses out of one his pockets and picked up a Bible on the table beside him. "I want to turn your attention to the good book now. I know that's where I turn whenever I'm... confused or lost, and I hope that y'all do the same. I'm gonna read a little bit here I like from Ephesians, 4:31." His voice turned even more booming as he read aloud, "'Get rid of all bitterness, passion, and anger. No more shouting or insults, no more hateful feelings of any sort. Instead, be kind and tenderhearted to one another, and forgive one another, as God has forgiven you through Christ.' Here's another one I like," he said, furiously turning pages. "Luke 23:34, 'Jesus said, "Forgive them, Father, for they know not what they do!"'" They know not what they do," he repeated pensively.

The pastor paused. "We are like children compared to the Almighty. No, no, not even that. We are beasts, animals, insects. But God has forgiven us. And who among us can claim that they are wiser than the Lord? So, if the Lord can forgive our sins, why shouldn't we follow in His wisdom? For we all live at His mercy, and if we do go to Heaven, it is through His grace.

"What I'm going to ask you to do, ladies and gentlemen, is to forgive those who have wronged you and offer them a hand to lead them back to the light. And most of all, I'm going to ask you to forgive yourselves. Receive that love that God has given for you and do your best to spread it to others. Because that's what's it all about, isn't it? We are put on this Earth to love. People are always trying to make life so complicated, but that's all you need to know. That's what I believe, any-ways, that's what the Lord teaches me. That is our purpose in this life, here, today.

"And on that note, I won't bore y'all any long-er, let us shake hands and join each other in a nice brunch, shall we?"

There was a general rumbling in the hall as people began turning to each other, shaking hands, and exchanging a few words. Only one of the old men in front of them turned back to Brett and Preston. "Peace be with you," he said to Pres-ton as he reached out.

Preston shook his hand, nodding and saying, "Right on."

The man extended the same hand and another "Peace be with you" to Brett.

Brett smiled. "Thanks, dude, and uh... also with you."

The man returned the smile and turned away. Gradually, the congregation of perhaps a few dozen people got up and began shuffling out of the main hall and towards another room at the side. "Come on, dude," Brett said to Preston, ris-ing from the pew. "I'm starving."

The two joined the crowd of worshippers as they filed towards the feast. It became all the more noticeable that while most of the church-goers were dressed in suits and dresses, quaint if not somewhat musty looking, Preston wore his usual attire of jeans and a hoodie and Brett was still wearing his St. Louis merchandise from the day before. However, neither of them and only a few among the rest of the crowd regarded this as they marched into a large dining hall, with several buffet lines already set up and beckoning out to the starving masses.

Brett scrambled ahead, speeding past children and the elderly towards the buffet, while Preston hung back a little. He decided that he would begin by getting a coffee, and then circle back to the food once the lines had begun to dissipate. Everything was going according to plan, until he heard a voice behind him as he was putting cream and two sugars in his drink: the voice he had already been listening to for far longer than he had cared to. "Hello there, stranger," the preacher said.

Preston turned around to see him standing there, the only thing more slightly off white than his suit being the teeth he showed in a concerningly wide and friendly smile. "What's up, man?" Preston responded as he was stirring his coffee.

The preacher chuckled, obviously tickled by Preston's greeting, though Preston couldn't tell why in particular. "You can call me Pastor Freeman, or just Pastor, or Jefferson. Hell, you can call me Sally, I won't try to stop you." Once more he chuckled heartily.

"Preston," Preston identified himself, doing his best to move his tongue as little as possible since the first sip of coffee he took was like hellfire in his mouth, a pain he did he best to hide as he smothered his desire to scream.

"Preston," the pastor repeated, meditating on the word. "Where you from, Preston? Haven't seen you around before. And I'd remember."

"Why's that?"

"Because I think I've seen about three brothers since I moved here." He snickered, and this time Preston joined him.

"Uh…" Preston began. His muscles relaxed. He hadn't even realized that he had tensed them in the first place. "Me and my friend are coming from Vermont, Burlington."

"Vermont? Probably the only place you could find less black people than this town."

"Yeah," Preston scoffed. "And I'm the one actually from there, he's from Kansas City."

"Ah, the big KC," the pastor said with a smile, as Preston instantly scowled. "Your friend's called Brett, right? We got to talking back at the diner yesterday."

"Yeah, right, Brett. He was, uh, very enthusiastic about coming here."

"Oh really?"

"Yeah, yeah, he's very…" Preston looked over to see Brett with a hefty plate of food in hand, delicately attempting to balance a bagel on top of the already mountainous pile of food. "He's a spiritual type, you know?"

"I'm guessing you were less enthusiastic," the pastor said with a smile.

"Huh?"

"I saw you in the back row there. You looked like you were about to pass out."

Preston shrugged. "Not really my scene, I guess."

"I understand, trust me, I do. But might I suggest you do yourself a favor and at least give it a fair shot some time," he said in a low, intimate voice.

"Why do you care?" Preston surprised even himself with a tinge of hostility.

The preacher put on a grim straight face and stared at Preston for a moment. "Because I can see it in your eyes."

"See what?"

"The pain. The suffering. The depression, the self-loathing. I had the same eyes for a long time." Preston didn't really know how to respond to this. He wasn't particularly impressed at the pastor's insight; he figured that just about everyone felt those things and fancied themselves as fascinating people with hidden depth just waiting to be uncovered by a sagacious soul like this pastor because of it. After a brief pause, the pastor moved on. "So, what brings you two from Vermont to a drive-through town in a flyover state?"

"We're going west, California."

"Moving there or just visiting?"

Preston hesitated and took a moment to reflect on the fact that he hadn't the slightest idea of what his actual plan was. "Visiting," he finally stuttered out, deciding it would be the less suspicious answer.

The pastor noticed how he stumbled over this seemingly simple question, but decided not to press it any further. Another silence passed. "You mind if I ask you something?"

Preston did mind. "I guess not," he answered.

"What'd you think of my sermon today?" the pastor smiled affably.

"Uh... I don't know."

"You don't know what you thought?"

"Well, like I said, not really my scene," Preston answered. The pastor was still smiling at him, staring expectantly. Preston's eyes wandered off the pastor and settled on the floor as he shifted uncomfortably. "I guess- I don't know." Suddenly, Preston brought his eyes back up to meet the pastor's. The smile had dissolved, and they simply stared for an unending second. "Do you really believe all that shit you said in there?"

"I don't believe in the Lord, I *know* He is real."

"No, I get that, but… All that about forgiveness… You really think anyone, anything can be forgiven?"

"I think that those who repent *must* be forgiven."

Well, what the fuck does it mean to repent, Preston thought to himself.

"Tell me what's troubling you," the pastor said softly without any trace of the smile.

Preston didn't answer for a moment. "Well," he began, then paused again. "It's just that, I had this girlfriend and, uh… She died, just recently."

Preston had been expecting one of the lines he always heard, the "Oh, that's terrible," or the "I'm sorry for your loss," or "She's in a better place now," or perhaps the one he hated the most of all, "Everything happens for a reason."

But the pastor didn't say anything, merely watching Preston as he spoke. "How did it happen?" he asked when Preston didn't go on.

He had, of course, heard this question more than a few times. Still, it sent him spinning every time he heard it, a thousand places to put the blame passing through his mind every second.

There was one that always won out, that shouted louder than all the others. But instead, the words "It's, uh… It's kinda a long story," finally stumbled their way out of his lips. "But, She uh... She killed Herself."

"Ah," the pastor said. "I see what's the problem." He sighed through his nose for a moment. "You're wondering how Her soul will rest now that She's taken Her own physical life."

"No, I-"

"Well, as a pastor, it's my job to help my flock find the truth, so I'll be frank with you-"

"Seriously, I'm not- Just listen to-"

"There's nothing that can be done for your girlfriend's soul, I'm afraid."

Preston paused his objections, taken aback. "The fuck does that mean?"

"Well, I'm sure She was a fine girl, but She committed the one crime that can't be forgiven, that She can't repent. She rejected this great gift of life that God has given us. She defied His will. She claimed to know better than God. Now, I know, the temptation can be great in the darkest times, but-"

"So, what, She's in hell?" Preston raised his voice.

"Well-"

"What, you can forgive a murderer or a rapist or a fucking scumbag like yourself, but you can't let a dead girl off?"

"Calm yourself," the pastor said. "I want to help you, friend. I only know what God has told me."

"And what did God tell you in His infinite fucking wisdom, huh?"

"That your girlfriend committed a sin that can't be forgiven, and She'll be punished accordingly in the next life. Now-"

Preston didn't consciously choose his next action. It was more of a reflex when he lifted his arm and brought down a swift strike with the back of his hand across the pastor's face. If he had been fully in control of his actions, he also might have chosen a more elegant speech than simply screaming the word "Fuckface," as he did while bringing the hammer of his hand down. However, he could not deny the euphoric rush of satisfaction that came when he heard the smack of his hand meeting the pastor's face and the thud as he fell to the ground.

The dining hall went completely silent for a moment. An agonizingly long moment. A moment long enough for the wave of euphoria to subside in favor of an even more overwhelming wave of "Oh shit" repeating over and over in Preston's head.

"What the fuck, dude?" he heard Brett shouting from across the room.

It was this question thrown out to the heavens that jolted Preston into action once more. He broke out into a sprint, or at least his version of a sprint, which can perhaps best be described as a clumsy jog, towards the exit. Brett followed him, pushing aside the elderly churchgoers that were in his way and barreling through the church's hall in Preston's wake. Brett picked up a few hymn books and threw them behind him and knocked

119

over the altar in order to slow down their pursuers, despite the fact that no one else had even begun to leave the dining hall yet.

Brett burst through the doors of the church to see Preston already hopping into the Civic which was parked on the street outside. "What the fuck, dude?" he repeated, shouting. "You pimp slapped a priest!"

"I know, I know," Preston responded, hurriedly opening the driver's side door. "Just get in the car, man."

"Why did you pimp slap a priest?"

"I don't know, man, I don't know, it just happened."

"Pimp slapping a priest is a choice, dude, it doesn't just fucking happen." Brett reached the Civic and attempted to slide across the hood much as the hero of an action movie might, but he only made it about half way. He rolled down off the hood and ran the rest of the way, flinging the passenger door open and jumping in. "Hit the gas!" he shouted, even though Preston was now sitting right next to him.

It took Preston about twenty-seven seconds to get out of his parallel parking sandwiched between two cars. The congregation showed no signs of pursuing them, but still when he was finally free, he pressed the gas hard enough for the tires to squeal as the Civic peeled down the road, away from the church.

3

The night had come, and Preston had left the Civic and Brett back at the rest stop a small distance behind him, a glowing hilltop housing a small fleet of vehicles. He was standing beneath the stars and the treetops in the woods at the side of the road, the only light that of a cigarette hanging loosely in his mouth. He didn't really smoke, or at least he didn't used to. He didn't like the taste. Or the smell. Or the cancer. But Ophelia did. He hated that She smoked, ironically enough. Out of all the shit that they did together, all the poisons they shared, that was the one thing he tried to get Her to quit. And now the smell reminded him of Her and of the times they spent loitering outside Her dorm, talking just to hear each other speak. Those were the moments he missed the most. He loved their highs, and even their lows in a certain way, but it was the day to day simplicities that he couldn't fathom going on without Her. He didn't know how time passed anymore. It simply did. The hours and the days bled into one another until it was all a vague blur of numb pain and longing. And now, smoking gave him the perfect excuse to be outside and alone with Her ghost, even for a moment.

Preston was halfway through his cigarette when he felt a buzz in his pocket. He whipped his phone out, the screen lighting up like one of the stars in the vast canvas of the night sky above the treetops. Dalia was calling him. He had almost forgotten their appointment.

"Hey," he said into the phone as he tossed down the cigarette and stamped out the flame.

"Hey," she replied. Then after a second of pause, "How was your day?"

"Uh…" He let out a thick cough or two. "Well, it was interesting, definitely."

"Oh yeah?"

"Yeah, yeah."

A pause. "What made it so interesting?"

Preston sighed. "I'll tell you one day."

"Why not today?"

"Well, it's part of a… you know, a developing situation."

"Really?" she sounded unconvinced.

"It'll make a better story once I can tell you the full, uh, arc of it, you know?"

"Oh, well, I suppose I shall trust your storytelling prowess, then."

"Thank you, thank you."

The night was silent. It had begun snowing. Just a little. Probably the first snows in these parts, drifting down in a gentle little dance. "So…" Dalia said eventually.

"So," he repeated, reluctant to break the silence.

"How've you been?"

"Oh, never better."

"Seriously, Preston."

"I- I, uh… Well, I've been worse."

"That's not saying much, is it?"

"No, not really."

"Come on, talk to me. What's the matter?"

Preston took a few steps, pacing around the woods, one hand stuffed deep in his jacket pocket, the other holding the phone to his ear. "Can I ask you something kinda weird?"

"Go for it."

It took him a moment before he could work up the courage to go for it. "Do you, uh… You believe in… the afterlife or any of that shit?"

She hesitated for a moment. "Can't say that I do to be honest." She quickly started again, "I don't mean to-"

"No, no. I… don't really either. Never bought into all that. My dad always said he didn't believe in taking anything on faith. My mom took me to her church a couple times when I was little but it just… never stuck for some reason."

"Some people are just not… predisposed to it, I think. I never had the time or the patience to think about the little things like God."

"Fair enough, I guess."

"You're asking because of Her," she stated.

"Uh… Yeah, I guess that's it. I just- I hate that nothing can change now. It's like we're just stuck in one of Her bad days forever. I can't tell Her I love Her anymore. I can't fix anything. I can't… I can't tell Her I'm sorry."

"Sorry for what?" Silence. "Sorry for what, Preston?"

Preston felt tears filling his eyes. "I killed Her," his voice came out in a weak crack. "I fucking killed Her, Dalia."

"Don't say that."

"I did, I fucking killed Her, I killed Her, I fuck-ing-"

"Preston," she raised her voice over his break-down. "Preston, calm down."

"I don't want to calm down," he cried. His heart was pounding like a snare drum, his mouth had gone completely dry while his eyes watered and his nose filled with mucus. "People have been telling me to calm down the last six months, like everything's fucking okay, but it's not, it's all fucked."

"Preston-"

"It's fucked, I'm fucked."

"Slow down, just… Just tell me what's wrong."

Preston's hands were shaking. He felt sweat running down his face despite the fact that it was freezing cold, and snowflakes kept prickling his skin. He took a few shaky, deep breaths. "I was- I was in a church today, you know, and it just… Just totally brought me back to the funeral. All those people just standing around, even Her mom, I could just hear them thinking 'Oh, this is sad, but it was always gonna happen, She was the crazy girl.' I wanted to just grab them all and scream 'It's my fault, She didn't do anything wrong.' It didn't- it didn't have to happen. It wouldn't've if…" his voice trailed off.

"If what?"

"It was the fucking drugs that did it. I got Her into all that shit. It's my fault."

"There's no use talking like that, Preston."

"She's dead because of me. She'd be alive if She never knew me. How am I supposed to live with that?"

"You don't know that."

He was sobbing now. His fists clenched until his knuckles turned as white as the paper of his cigarettes. "Why wasn't I enough?"

"Preston."

"I never would've left Her like that, so why-"

"Because no one's ever 'enough,' Preston. You can't fix another person, that's just-... that's not how it works. It's not your fault, it's not anyone's fault, it's just… shitty."

"Everyone would just be better off without me."

"That's not true."

"How would you know?" Preston snapped.

"Because, I'd miss you."

"Really?"

"I like our thing, Preston. I feel like I'm… I feel like I'm not alone, even if it's just for a few moments a day."

Preston paused and listened to the silence. "Dalia," he finally said.

"What?"

"Have you ever been in love?"

"What? Why would you ask me that?"

"I don't know, I guess I was just- I was wondering If I ever have. If I'm even… capable of that. It's all just chemicals in the brain and all that, you know? So, there's gotta be some people that just… don't, can't, whatever. Just not meant for that shit. And I mean, I think that I loved Ophelia but... I don't know, I don't know. I guess if love is so fucking great, and I really genuinely did love Her, then, you know, why did She...? Even with you, it's like-"

"Preston, I need to go."

"What? What do you mean?"

"I need to go."

"Wait, Dali, why-"

She hung up.

He didn't drop the phone from his ear for a moment.

She hung up.

His arm collapsed to his side and he looked at the blank screen. What did he do wrong? Had he finally fucked up the last thing that he had? She had finally gotten tired of him, of his asinine melodrama, of his attachment to a woman he had never even seen. He almost told her that he loved her, but how could he? What the hell was he doing out here anyway? Everything he had done since she picked up the phone that one night now seemed to lie somewhere on a scale between utterly stupid and psychotic.

But he couldn't get abandoned now. There were people that genuinely did care about him. But they were all behind him now. And she was ahead.

Preston brought the phone up to his ear once more as he tried to call her again, only to listen to the ring laughing at him, only to hear the robotic female voice of a voicemail on the other end. He repeated the process a few times, each time his heart pounding harder, the pulse reverberating in his ears. His hands were shaking, his mouth had gone completely dry. He began to feel the chill.

Finally, he lowered his phone and looked at the blank screen. He grabbed a fistful of his hair and clenched his fists and his eyes shut. "Fuck," he whispered.

4

"Are you ready for the greatest experience of your life, dude?" Brett's voice joined the legion that was already swimming through Preston's head.

From behind the tinted lenses of his sunglasses Preston looked at a monument of human gluttony and pride. What stood before the two was an American Ozymandias, a titan of capitalist achievement. About the height of three men stacked on top of each other, or approximately four and a half men with dwarfism, was a giant orb of LED lights vaguely resembling the Earth, though it did admittedly take a few geographical liberties that were inexcusable. Even in the evening sun, the lights were nearly blinding. Scrawled across the globe in garish hot pink was the run-on sentence of a name "Adventure Fun World and Water Fun World: The Crown Jewel of KC!"

Standing next to the globe, with one arm draped around the top, was the imposing figure of an anthropomorphic fox, wearing what appeared to be the clothes of some sort of sailor, a frighteningly enthusiastic grin, and a crown on top of his head. "Okay," Preston began. "I get the crown thing, with the slogan and all, but what the fuck is with the rest of this guy?"

"That's King Fred the Fox," Brett grinned.

"If he's like, you know, a monarch, why is he dressed like a pirate?"

Brett shrugged and looked up at the giant along with Preston. "They were going for an adventurer type theme, I think."

"And why the shit is he a fox?"

"I don't know, for the kids."

"I feel like that would be terrifying to a kid. Fuck, man, I'm an adult and I feel terrified."

Brett walked up to the goliath. "The children of Kansas City are a hardy people, dude. I loved this guy when I was little." He patted the monster's leg and smiled wistfully. After a moment of silent nostalgia, he turned back to Preston. "Come on, dude. Time to take your Adventure Fun World and Water Fun World virginity."

"You know what, man, I'm, uh… I'm not feeling so up to it, I'd just slow you down."

"What's the matter?"

Preston hesitated. "I just-"

"Oh my god, dude, are you dying?"

"No, Brett, I'm not fucking dying, I'm just not in the mood for a goddamn amusement park, okay?"

"Oooh," Brett recoiled. "Someone's cranky. You know what the best way to get… not cranky? Adventure. And fun. And water. And worlds."

"It's fucking December, I don't know why a water park is even open, let alone why you would want to go in one."

"The risk of hypothermia is the best part, dude. Adventure!"

"No, no adventure, Brett."

"Look, we don't have to go on the water rides. To be honest, Adventure Fun World is far superior to Water Fun World."

"No, Brett, I don't want to go to any Fun Worlds."

"I don't think you understand, dude."

"I underst-"

"This is the best theme park in America, dude. They have an international theme, the likes of which have never been seen-"

"You mean like Epcot?"

"No, dude, not at all like Epcot."

"It sounds like Epcot."

"Adventure Fun World and Water Fun World," Brett was raising his voice, attracting the attention of the small crowd entering the park in the middle of the winter on a weekday, "is to Epcot as fine dining in Rome is to Papa John's, dude."

"Okay, just calm down."

Brett continued, "They have a section of the park for America, Europe, the Amazon, the Orient-"

"The fuck is the Orient?"

"You know, the, uh- the Eastern world."

"Was this park made by a 19th century British Imperialist?"

"Adventure Fun World was founded in 1918, and it was just the push America needed to make it through the Great War-"

"What the fuck are you talking about?"

"I'm talking about a piece of Americana here, dude."

"Ameri-" Preston stopped himself from shouting. "I'm going to the fucking Civic, I'm gonna take a drive, have fun."

He began to turn back towards the parking lot, when Brett called back after him. "Preston Dwayne Carter-"

"That's not even my middle name."

"I have Josh Groban's entire discography on CD in my duffle bag back in the civic. If you do not step into Adventure Fun World and Water Fun World right now, that's all we're listening to for the rest of the trip."

"You wouldn't dare," Preston glared at him.

"You know I would. What do you have against the Grob?"

"He's a smug bastard."

"Come on, this is slander. He has the voice of an angel."

"He sounds like gentrification."

"Your hatred for him is just ridiculous."

"I don't hate him, he's not significant enough to hate, he doesn't stand for anything."

"We've been through this-"

"Why did you bring his entire discography?" Preston cried.

"I always have an exit strategy, dude. I know your weaknesses."

"Fucking- ugh, fine."

"Nice," Brett smiled, victorious. "You are not gonna regret this, dude."

"I already do."

Still, Preston followed Brett through the park's gates and into the maw of the beast of fun. A grim frown crossed his face as he marched through the entryway, sandwiched between grinning children and Brett, whose face was lit up with a rapturous, sickening ecstasy. The death march proceeded as one by one, legions of sticky children and slightly overweight and extremely exhausted parents were admitted into the park. Finally, he and Brett came to the front of the line, and they each purchased a ticket and received a stamp on their hand from an apathetic employee. She didn't even wait for Preston to prepare for the stamp, merely slapping it in his palm as he received the ticket. Brett was more prepared, and promptly stuck out the back of his hand to receive the proper stamp placement.

Brett's description of the park was confirmed by a sign right in front of the park's entry way, with arrows pointing towards America, the Amazon, Europe, and the Orient, each written in its own characteristic, vaguely politically incorrect font. Brett insisted that they begin with America and save the Orient for their grand finale. Preston begrudgingly obliged. There was a constant thin and wispy, obnoxiously low hanging cloud over America. It originated from, Preston presumed, a small section called "The Rocket's Red Glare," which promised a patriotic firework display, but in reality, consisted of a few bored employees setting off firecrackers in a desperate attempt to amuse themselves.

The first ride they went on was the second largest rollercoaster in the park, behind only The

Chinese Dragon located in the Orient. It was called "The Yankee." Preston assumed that it was meant to be themed around Abraham Lincoln, though the only real indication of this was a series of tall, stovepipe top hats decorating the rails on the line up to the ride. Preston couldn't focus on the endless tirade of historical context of the park and each significant ride that Brett spewed out of his mouth as they waited in line. His mind was filled with smoke and haze. His body felt like a sack of dead flesh hanging on his frame. His eyes kept focusing on the grains in the asphalt walkways.

Preston had only been on a few rollercoasters in his life and had been to even fewer amusement parks, mostly with his brother when he was a teenager and Preston was still a kid that he was sick of. Back then, he remembered enjoying the rides. But today, the climbs and the drops, the seat belt digging into his stomach, the bar pressing into his chest, it all seemed like an exercise in futility and nausea. At times, he felt a pang of guilt for his lethargic anhedonia and the obvious disappointment it caused Brett. That is, until Brett opened his mouth.

No, he didn't to want to go into the Gorilla Kingdom in the Amazon section, frankly he didn't think that there even were gorillas in the entire Amazon. No, Brett, he couldn't guarantee that there wasn't one gorilla in the Amazon, but there sure as shit wasn't a whole goddamn kingdom, and no, that wasn't just his opinion.

And the Haunted Palace was not a historically accurate representation of the daily life of medieval French nobility. Because there were fucking ghosts, Brett.

Brett had more or less learned to be quiet by the time night had long fallen and they had made it through most of the Orient. The only behemoth left for them was the Chinese Dragon, whose rickety legs seemed to stretch endlessly into the sky, illuminated by floodlights. For a moment, they stood on the ground below it, watching as the rollercoaster cars with wooden sidings carved into the shape of a dragon and covered with a vibrant, if not slightly chipped, layer of vermillion paint came barreling down the hills. After a few rounds of this, Brett finally turned to Preston. "Are you ready, dude?"

"Why don't you take this one without me?" Preston mumbled.

"Come on, dude."

"Seriously, I'm not feeling it."

"Don't be like that."

"You know what, I wasn't really feeling any of this but I still fucking went-"

"I do know, you made it very clear you weren't feeling it, dude."

"I still went with you, despite that, despite the fact that I feel like shit. I still went on The Yankee and the Rainforest Ride, and I played Whack the Charlie, which is definitely racist, by the way."

"I told you, that game was put in during Vietnam, it was a different time."

"But can you just give me this one break? I don't want to go on any more rides."

"You know, you haven't exactly been a great friend today, you were just fucking set on being as miserable as possible."

"Maybe because you're dragging me all over the place-"

"I just wanted to cheer you up, dude, share something that's important to my life, because that's what friends do."

"Maybe if you wanted to cheer me up, you should've just let me be."

"That's hurtful, dude, real fucking hurtful."

"Yeah, well... Fuck man, I'm in a bad mood and I just wish you would just respect that."

Brett paused. "I'm sorry, dude."

"Yeah, me too."

"You wanna go now?"

Preston looked up at the coaster towering above them. "Go on, give it a go."

Brett smiled before breaking out in a light jog to join the line up to the Dragon. Preston was left alone with his thoughts. He leaned on a railing and watched as the coaster flew and the line slowly marched forward. Brett gradually climbed up to the dragon and took his seat on its back, at the very front, of course. Preston for the first time that day wasn't at all irritated or dismissive at the sight of Brett's childlike, irrepressible grin as the coaster came shooting down the tracks. He even felt a pang of guilt. His eyes wandered off the coaster's path as he became lost in his mind, wondering why he couldn't just shut the fuck up and be a decent human being to the people that cared about him.

"Preston," a voice called him back to reality.

He snapped his head towards its source to find Brett standing there, a wide smile across his face and a long, dragon shaped plush toy draped around his neck. "Check it out, the ride got off right at the gift shop!"

Preston smiled. "That's a nice dragon, Brett."

He looked down on it with pride. "Yeah," he said, nodding. "Yeah, it is... Come on, let's hit the road, dude."

Together they walked out of the Orient and through the grand gates at the park's mouth, past King Fred the Fox, and into the night shrouded parking lot.

5

After leaving Adventure Fun World and Water Fun World, Preston felt a wave of serenity and contentment wash over the shores of his mind, a peace that had become scarce in recent months.

This lasted slightly less than twenty minutes.

Brett was driving the Civic west, toward Kansas. Aside from the symphony of mechanical, slightly worrying noises the Civic released while performing its basic operations, the car was silent. No music was rattling out of the speakers and there was no chatter between the two occupants. Preston flicked the car's radio on without much thought. "-ternational news today," a voice over the radio began, "reports are coming in that the rogue state has successfully tested missiles capable of the striking the entire continental United-" Preston reached out and turned the dial. "-rotests continue in the streets of Los Angeles and other major cities following the not guilty verdict in the case of the death of California teenager Lavar-" a different voice managed to get out before Preston turned the radio off entirely. Another silence passed.

Boredom overtook Preston, and he instinctively reached for his phone in response.

In his right pocket was his wallet. In his left, his keys to the Civic and their apartment. He felt his heart stop as he stuffed his hands into the pocket of his hoodie to find it empty. He went through each of the pockets once more. He even checked his back pockets, despite the fact that he couldn't remember a time in his life when he actually used them.

A few more increasingly desperate attempts to rifle through his pockets later, he moved on to the general area around him. He searched the floor, clawed at the cushion of his seat, checked the glove box to make sure that his phone hadn't gained the ability to travel through walls. All to no avail. Brett did his best to keep his eyes on the road, but he continuously glanced over at Preston. "What's the matter, dude?"

"My phone," Preston muttered.

"What?"

"My fucking phone, dude, I can't find it. Shit." He searched for a moment longer. "I definitely had it while we were in line for the... the fucking, you know-"

"The Yankee?"

"No, no, in, uh... In fucking Europe, man."

"Fantasy Castle?"

"Fantasy Castle, that's the one. Fuck me, I must have lost it on that."

"Shit, dude."

"We need to turn around," Preston said in a grave tone. "I need my fucking phone."

"Alright, alright. They might not even be open by the time we get there, though."

"Well, hurry up then, man."

After a small series of extremely questionable driving decisions, they were back on the path towards Adventure Fun World and Water Fun World. Preston's heart had climbed into his throat and he found himself pressing his foot to the Civic's floor as if he had his own gas pedal and could will Brett to drive even further beyond the speed limit. This continued until the car came to a halt roughly inside a space in the Adventure Fun Parking Lot and Water Fun Parking Lot. Preston hurriedly hopped out of the car and started marching towards the gates of the park, Brett lagging a bit behind.

The gates were guarded by two employees, one male and one female, both somewhere in their late teens, that had been there at least since Preston and Brett had originally come. The girl was on her phone and the boy standing awkwardly nearby. An older, portly man was sitting behind the glass screen of the ticket booth a short distance off, apparently their manager. As Preston stormed the gates, the girl spoke up. "You got a ticket?" she asked without looking up from her phone.

Preston held up the stamp on his hand, already slightly faded. "I was here earlier today."

The girl looked up at his hand, then went back to her phone. "Stamp's supposed to be on the back of your hand."

"You stamped it, I came through a few hours ago."

"I don't remember everyone who comes through here," she shrugged, too disinterested to really be defensive.

"Look, he's got his stamp," Preston indicated Brett, who promptly held up his own hand with a wide grin.

"Park's closed."

"What?"

"It's 9:43, park closed at 9:30."

"Why didn't you start with that?"

She shrugged again. "You didn't ask. Have an Adventure Fun Day," she said with an almost detectable attempt at enthusiasm.

The manager in the booth coughed loudly.

She sighed. "And a Water Fun Day."

"Look, I lost my phone on the Fantasy Castle, can I just real quick go look for it?"

"Park's closed."

"Just like, ten min-"

"She said park's closed, buddy," the boy suddenly shouted through a voice crack. "Back off."

"I need my phone, man."

The boy lowered his voice but maintained the same intensity. "Then you can fill out a Lost Item Form, either here in person or later on our website, and we'll look into your inquiry for the next four to five business days... bitch."

"Patrick," the manager scolded. "Language."

"Sorry sir," the boy said to Preston, but immediately after he mouthed the word "Bitch" again.

"I don't have four to fucking five business days, man, we need to-" It was here that Preston realized he was becoming that guy. That guy who yells at sixteen-year-old customer service workers. "Whatever, thanks."

The two started wandering back towards the parking lot. "Sorry about your phone, dude," Brett said. "We'll get you a burner or something."

"I don't want a fucking burner, dude, I need *my* phone."

"Look, we'll just fill out the form, if they find it we can have them send it to Uncle Quade in Anaheim, we'll pick it up when we get there."

"No, I can't fucking- I need it now," Preston raised his voice.

"Just calm down, du-"

"Don't tell me to calm down, this wouldn't've happened if your dumb ass didn't drag us here."

"Oh, here we go again-"

"How do we get in?" Preston asked.

"What?"

"Come on, you gotta know some way to sneak in."

"Preston Sean Carter-"

"That's still not my middle name."

"I am an upstanding citizen, and a patron of local businesses."

"You never snuck in, not even once in all the fucking years you've been coming here?"

"Once, on a date, but then she dumped me at the top of the Ferris wheel and I spent the rest of the night crying on rollercoasters and eating fried dough until I threw up. I took it as bad karma, and I swore I would never purloin from the good people of Adventure Fun World and Water Fun World again."

"We already fucking patronized them, you idiot," Preston said, holding up his stamped hand. "There's, like, no moral ambiguity."

Brett nodded slowly. "Cogent," he said. "Don't appreciate the tone, but cogent."

"Come on then, man."

Brett pushed out ahead and lead him around the edges of the park, along a chain link fence. Soon they passed from the streetlights of the parking lot into the shadows of the trees. "This was like eight years ago, dude," Brett said. "I don't know if this will still work."

"It better."

"I'm just saying, no promises."

"Jesus fucking Christ," Preston mumbled. "We're getting the phone, one way or another."

Suddenly Brett stopped in his tracks. "Alright, here we are, dude."

Preston wasn't entirely sure what he had been expecting, aside from perhaps some kind of breach in the fencing. But the chains stood as resolute as ever, taller than the two of them combined. "Where's here?" Preston said.

"This is definitely the place," Brett answered. "Look at that," Brett indicated two knots in a nearby tree that sat right next to each other. "I remember it was the tree that looked like it had balls," he chuckled.

Preston paused for a moment, then his voice returned with a slight edge of anger. "I'm sorry, I'm not seeing the relevance of the tree's balls."

"Well, we climbed the tree," Brett pointed up the trunk, "then we kinda shimmied along that branch there over the fence and just... hopped down."

"Seriously?"

Brett nodded.

"I didn't know there was gonna be fucking parkour involved," Preston whinged, though even as he whinged he was already approaching the tree and finding his footing on one of its balls.

"You love shimmying, dude."

"I've never shimmied in my goddamn life," Preston called down as he reached the branches of the tree and began shimmying towards the top of the fence.

"Clearly," Brett shouted up from the ground. "That's some shoddy shimmying, dude. More of a shuffle than anything."

"Yeah, well, why don't you-" Preston was towards the end of the branch, just past the fence, and was planning his route back down to the ground when he was cut off by a foreboding, haunting creek. He had just enough time to think to himself, Oh shit.

But before he could verbalize that thought, he heard the snapping of a branch and felt a drop worse than all the rollercoasters he had been subjected to. Especially since this particular drop actually ended with an impact, although admittedly this was still only slightly worse than the choruses of children and Brett screaming. As he crashed into the ground below, he let out a sound which, after long deliberation, has been declared impossible to recreate through text.

"Oh shit, dude," Brett said after a few seconds, apparently only just processing what had happened. "Are you okay?"

"Yeah," Preston groaned, although it was events such as these that seemed to emphasize the fact that he hadn't been okay in quite some time, if ever. "Never better."

"I told you, that was some poor shimmying. This tree's fucked, dude," Brett said. For the moment, Preston dared not move from the position he had landed in, staring up from his back at the broken branch and the stars beyond. From that perspective, the tree did indeed seem fucked. "Hold on, I'll go find a different tree."

"No, no, no," Preston interrupted. "Just... Wait in the Civic. You'll be the getaway driver."

"Are you sure, dude?"

"Yeah... Just go."

"Do you know how to get around the park?"

"I can figure it out.'

"Do we have an exit strategy here?"

"Let's just... Let's play it by ear, you know."

"If you insist, dude. I'll be in the parking lot, if you do find your phone intact, text me."

"Will do," Preston groaned. He still hadn't gotten up from his back.

"You good, dude?"

"Yeah, yeah, I'm just... resting."

"Cool, cool." Brett paused awkwardly for a second. "Well, I'm gonna go."

"Yup."

"Alright... I believe in you, dude. But don't get caught, I don't wanna get arrested. Or worse, banned from the park."

And with that, Preston listened to twigs and leaves crunching underneath the weight of Brett's step, slowly growing more and more distant until they were no longer audible. Okay, he thought, time to get up now. So, he remained on the ground for another moment. Now it was really time to get up.

His limbs and his back screamed in protest as he rose to a sitting position, and he let out another indescribable noise. He spent another minute resting once he had sat up, reconsidering all the life choices that had led him to this point. Then, he arose to his feet with an ever so slightly less excruciating pain. He stretched and sighed heavily before he started ambling in a direction that seemed correct.

When he emerged into the park itself, he was somewhere in America, star spangled banners lining the street in front of him, the Yankee just out of sight in the distance. There's something mystical about a closed amusement park: the crowds vanished, the lights out, the rides slumbering like great leviathans. Preston was left unattended in a child's dream world. However, he had neither the time nor the patience to appreciate the fact. His heart was still pounding. He couldn't get his mind off the image of her, or at least the woman he had imagined with her voice, desperately trying to call him and listening to his voicemail over and over again.

He prowled the streets of America, lit only by a full moon hanging low in the cloudless sky. He tried to move as quietly as he could, taking slow and gentle steps on the asphalt despite being fairly certain that all the employees had either already completely vacated the premises or were so apathetic as to make nothing of the deafening crashing that the breaking branch had produced on his way down. Still, he was self-conscious of the sound of his sneakers smacking against the pavement, and so stealth gave him a little peace of mind if nothing else.

The pilgrimage over to Europe was relatively uneventful, almost maddeningly so in fact. Shortly, he stood before Fantasy Castle. Rollercoaster tracks twisted like a serpent around a small replica of a medieval castle, with a mannequin dressed in cheap plastic chainmail and wielding a wooden sword and shield standing below on the ground and a dragon perched on one of the castle's towers. There was another mannequin, this one vaguely feminine and draped in a purple dress, looking out a window high up in the castle, apparently a princess awaiting her savior below. Preston got on the empty ramp leading up to the sleeping ride, then hopped over the railing onto the grass below.

He wandered through the unmowed, dewy grass for a few minutes, through the castle's courtyard. He followed the shadows of the tracks, his eyes to the ground carefully inspecting every blade of grass and every object lying amidst them. His heart nearly leapt out of his chest at the sight of a few rocks that from a distance looked vaguely like a smartphone in just the right light. Checking every loop and turn on the coaster's path got him no closer to finding it. He had nearly given up hope when he finally saw it.

Lying there at the knight's feet, in the shadow of his sword.

Even from a distance he could see one of its lights faintly blinking, telling him it wasn't irreparably destroyed and he even had a message. He broke out into an awkward sort of light jog towards the knight. His fingers were trembling as he picked up the phone, the screen slightly more cracked than it already was but otherwise still intact. He wiped the dew off with the sleeve of his hoodie.

Thirteen missed calls. None of them went to voicemail. All of them from Dalia.

He scrambled to unlock his phone and lifted it up to his ear. "One. Saved. Message," a robotic female voice announced. "June. Twenty fifth." A long, atonal beep as he felt his stomach churning and closed his eyes. "Hey there," She said, Her voice light and playful, Her cadence bouncy. "Call me back, fuckface."

He lowered the phone to close his eyes and exhale for a moment. Then, he brought it back up to call Dalia back. It was cold enough to see his breath and to feel his fingers crying out in pain, but he was sweating. The phone rang. And it rang again.

Dalia picked up the call, but she didn't say anything for a moment. "Dalia?" Preston said. "Are you okay?"

All Preston could hear was a faint, fast sort of tapping, like fingers rolling on a snare drum or a heavy rain. "You fu-" her voice came suddenly. "You fucked me up the other night Preston."

"Yeah, well. You kinda fucked me up too."

"I'm sorry, I'm sorry, I just-" she let out a sort of half sigh half groan. "No, you know what, I'm not sorry, you're the one who brought up all that fucking bullshit."

"What? Are you drunk?"

147

"Yes, I'm fucking drunk. I'm… fucking- I'm fucking sitting at the bottom of my shower with a bottle of vodka. Because you brought up all that love shit, I'm not good with that shit."

"You think I am?"

She was crying.

She was crying.

Preston heard it but he couldn't really wrap his mind around the concept.

"I'm fucking everything up and I can't- I can't stop it. I'm just a huge piece of shit to everyone that could possibly care about me."

"You haven't been a piece of shit to me."

"Yes, I have," she was sobbing. "I've just been taking advantage of you."

"Is this about the book?" Preston asked.

She didn't say anything, she just kept sobbing into the phone.

"Dalia," Preston began again. He had been pacing around the knight and was now wandering over to sit on the edge of a moat just before the castle, which was really more of an empty, shallow ditch. "I don't care about the fucking book anymore."

"Yeah, well, maybe you should care. Maybe you should have some goddamn self-respect."

"We're way past the point of no return on that."

She started laughing. He joined her. Then there was only the beating of the shower for a moment. "I like hearing you tell me I'm good," Dalia eventually said through an audible smirk.

"You're good, Dalia," a similar smirk crept across Preston's face.

"I almost believe you when you say it like that."

"Oh yeah?"

"Yeah… It almost makes me forget that we don't know each other."

"I'd say we've gotten to know each other a little."

"You know what I mean." More silence. "I wish you did know me," she eventually said in slurred words. "I wish you were here."

"Me too," he said. "Maybe… Maybe I could be there one day."

"Maybe," she repeated.

Preston noticed that the mesmerizing white noise of the shower on the other end of the line had stopped. Something about this reminded him that he was currently trespassing on the private property of an amusement park and had already left Brett unattended far longer than it was wise to. "I think I have to go this time. Are you sure you're okay?"

"Can't you stay with me a bit longer? We don't have to say anything, just… just stay on the line. Just for a minute or two."

Preston looked around, making sure he was alone. The pitch black of the night had settled down over the park.

The castle was the only thing he could see.

"Alright." He muttered. "It'll be alright."

Nevada

1

There's something about nights in a city. Dwarfing might be a word for it, but that's not nearly enough. Manmade mountains are draped in hundreds of lights, each one a window, a beacon of a life. A person. A story. The mass accumulation of human experience is on full display, defying the dusk and the darkness with radiance, creating thousands of their own stars. And all the stars, whether the size of a phone screen or a streetlight or a neon sign, has its own solar system orbiting it. The city becomes a universe of its own. The only thing easier than getting completely, utterly lost in the galaxy of individuals is anchoring yourself to other people, each connection more convoluted and obscure and unexplainable than the next. Then of course comes the realization that everything that preceded this moment, the sum of your experience, you yourself, are just another star in the darkness. And you are endowed with a crippling liberation. There's an infinity of possibility and totality of freedom with an apparent impossibility of having true consequence.

And there's something more about nights in Las Vegas.

Admittedly, this urban sublime which Preston might have experienced from the driver's seat of the Civic was somewhat spoiled when he managed to catch a glimpse of two rats fucking on the sidewalk with a third scurrying off from a trash can with what he could only guess to be a chunk of a moldy bagel. He did his best to avoid this sight as he and Brett sat in a long line of cars behind a red light, and distracted himself by checking the gas on the dashboard. "We should hit the next gas station," he announced.

"Do what you gotta do," Brett responded.

There was a pause, music on the stereo and distant honking horns filling the air. "Hey," Preston spoke up again. "We gotta go to the Strip, right?"

Brett shifted in his seat and didn't meet Preston's expectant eyes. "We don't *gotta* do anything."

"Come on, we're in Vegas."

"I am well aware of our geographical location, my dude, that doesn't mean we have to spend tonight throwing away my money."

"Look, we don't actually have to gamble or anything, we don't have to go in a fucking casino, I just wanna see it, maybe get a few drinks. Furthest west I've been is Detroit before this. I gotta see the sights, you know."

"You didn't want to see Adventure Fun World and Water Fun World, what's got you so adventurous now?"

"I was in a bad mood, I just wanted to sit in the Civic and get drunk. Now I'm in a good mood, I just want to go out and get drunk."

"Look, I'm not saying anything, I'm just saying there's a lot of potential for trouble on the Strip. If we're gonna get drunk, let's get drunk in a relatively low risk environment."

"Don't be a fucking nerd, man-"

"I am not a nerd."

"You're being one right now."

"No, no-"

"Strip, Strip, Strip, Strip," Preston began chanting. He glanced out his window to see an elderly woman on the sidewalk, giving him a foul look. "Oh, no, not you, ma'am, I'm chanting at my friend here."

The woman began scuttling down the street, clenching her coat and hanging her head with a look of rage and disgust. "See where your hedonism is getting us?" Brett said.

"You're one to lecture me about fucking hedonism."

"Hey, I'll partake, but I'll do so in a controlled, safe manner."

"Oh yeah, you were real safe on Halloween."

"I don't even remember that night."

"Yeah, that's my point."

"That was like a month and a half ago anyways, I'm a new man."

"Oh, oh, I'm real sorry, nice to meet you, sir," Preston said as the light turned green and the Civic began rollicking forward once again. "Dumbass," he muttered. "Look, we gotta find some gas first. We'll do that, grab some snacks-"

"Don't try to bribe me with snacks-"

"We'll grab some snacks," Preston repeated, driving and scanning the streets for a station.

153

"And then we'll... you know, we'll figure out what we're doing."

"Alright, alright, whatever, dude."

It only took a few minutes of patrolling the streets of Las Vegas before they came to a gas station. Once he pulled up at a pump and filled the Civic's tank, he lent down to Brett's open window. "I'm gonna go in. Skittles?"

Brett looked beyond him, pensively taking in the city. "Nah," he answered after a brief silence. "Today's not a 'taste the rainbow' kinda day."

"Well, what do you want?"

Again, Brett paused. "You think they got gelato in there?"

"I sincerely doubt that they have gelato at this gas station."

"I could really go for some gelato," Brett mused, slowly nodding.

"Well, again... You got any other ideas?"

"Something low key, you know?"

"No," Preston said. "No, I don't know what it means for a snack to be low key."

"Low key, you know."

"I'm familiar with the phrase, but I don't see how it applies to- Do you consider gelato low key?"

Brett sighed heavily. "I'll come in with you."

He stepped out of the car and they headed into the convenience store attached to the station. The bell above the door rang merrily as they entered, starkly contrasting the instant wave of depression that comes with dim fluorescent lights and tile floors late at night. Brett prowled the aisles, searching for his snack of choice. Preston wasn't particularly hungry, but he did the same. He was deep among the protein bars when he suddenly heard Brett calling out from a few aisles away, "Oh shit!" and then laughing with a wheeze that marked it as his genuine, deep, full body laugh.

He tiptoed towards the outburst and peaked around the corner into the aisle. He saw Brett standing with, or, perhaps more accurately, beneath a towering, lanky, black man dressed in a faded red Mr. Rogers sweater over a white t shirt and jeans. There was something in the man's face that instantly reminded Preston of his brother, despite the fact that this man had darker skin and was much taller. So much so that Preston felt his heart leap into his throat as he rounded the corner and he had to resist the urge to simply flee. The man was carrying a case of beer in each hand. Brett turned around to see Preston peeking, and said, with a full grin, "Hey, Preston, it's Cal."

Preston came around the corner, a look of confusion stuck on his face. "Hi Cal," he waved cautiously.

"Hey," Cal replied. "I'm Cal."

"Y-Yeah, I'm Preston."

"Hey, Preston."

"Hi."

"I went to high school with this guy, he was my plug," Brett interjected.

"Brett was a damn good customer."

"Yeah, I bet," Preston said, taking a few steps forward to join the two.

"What's brings you to Vegas?" Brett asked.

"I live here now. This is where life is, huh?"

"Right on, man, that's what I'm trying to tell this guy," Preston said, whacking Brett on the arm.

"Aww, don't tell me you're a good Christian boy now, Brett."

"Uh… I'd say more of a morally ambiguous Agnostic."

"You still out in Vermont?" Cal asked.

"Yeah, yeah, we've been driving to Anaheim, started in Burlington."

"Shit, dude, nice," Cal laughed. "Hey, did you guys go through the big KC?"

"You know it."

"Did you stop at Adventure Fun World and Water Fun World?"

"Of course." Brett gestured towards Preston. "It was this guy's first time."

"Really? How'd you like it?"

Preston shrugged. "It was cool."

"He was fucking miserable," Brett laughed.

"How can you be miserable in that place?"

"He's a fucking contrarian, dude."

"I'm not a contrarian. Surly, maybe, but I'm not a fucking contrarian."

Another figure emerged from the sea of snack foods, carrying a bottle of vodka in each hand. She wasn't terribly small, but she was dwarfed standing next to Cal. She was white, with dirty blonde hair, and wore an oversized denim jacket over a black hoodie and a short skirt. "Who're these guys?" she asked.

"He's Brett," Cal said.

"I'm Brett."

"And that's Preston."

"What's up?" Preston said.

"Huh," the woman said. "Cool."

"This is Erin," Cal indicated the woman.

"I'm Erin."

"She's my twin sister." Preston and Brett stared at the two blankly. "Fraternal, obviously. Sometimes people call us Yin and Yang."

"Okay," Preston said. "Which one's which?"

"I don't think it really matters," Cal said with a shrug and a smile.

"Sorry, uh…" Brett began, pointing at Erin.

"I'm Erin," Erin said.

"Erin, right. Did you go to our high school? I don't remember you."

"Nah," Erin answered.

"We were separated at birth," Cal explained. "I didn't meet her till I moved here."

"So, uh… How'd you, uh…" Brett said. "How'd you know you were twins?"

Cal shrugged again. "Sometimes you just know, you know?"

"No," Preston answered.

"Right, know." Cal said, nodding with sagacity. Before either Preston or Brett could begin to unravel this web of a conversation, Cal moved on. "Hey, you guys need a place to party tonight? We got a place, right near the Strip, we're having a couple people over tonight. It's gonna be fun."

"That sound like the kinda shady shit we're looking for," Preston said, mostly to Brett.

"Come on, Brett," Cal urged him. "Old times sake?"

Brett paused. "Alright, alright."

157

There was a general sort of cheer between Cal and Preston, with Erin watching on silently from a slight distance. Cal patted Brett on the back and they all exited the store together. "Aren't you guys gonna pay for those?" Brett asked, indicating the drinks.

"Nah," Erin answered.

"Owner's an old friend," Cal said.

"Cool, cool," Brett replied, slightly unsure if it was actually cool.

"You guys wanna follow us or something?" Cal asked.

"Sure, yeah, we're in the Civic right there," Preston said.

Cal and Erin hopped into an old, beat up, maroon minivan parked just in front of the store and led the Civic out into the streets once more. It only took a brief moment for Brett and Preston to break the silence once they were out on the roads. "So, the twin thing…" Preston began.

"I don't even know, dude."

"Was he kidding?"

"I- I don't know much about twins but I feel like that's not… how *that* works."

"Whatever, dude, let's just- let's ignore that aspect and get really fucked up."

"Sounds like a plan."

They followed the van, navigating the streets and inching bit by bit closer to the Strip. Eventually, the Civic and the van pulled up to a bungalow on the corner of two streets. From the Civic, Preston could see that the front door was open, and the small crowd that had assembled inside the bungalow was spilling out onto the fairly spacious lawn. He could also hear, or rather, he could feel music emanating from the inside, the bass rumbling like the voice of a Lovecraftian beast. Preston, Brett, and the twins got out of their vehicles and approached the bungalow. They walked over a few people who were simply lying in the grass, staring at the stars, seemingly completely unperturbed by their presence or the existence of any other matter. On the porch, there was a small circle of people draped over cheap patio furniture or the porch's railings or simply the floorboards, a few blunts making their way around.

Yin and Yang stopped at the open doorway. "Well, boys, help yourselves," Cal said with a smile and a shrug, his hands buried in the pockets of his sweater. "Pick your poisons."

He walked into the bungalow, Erin slinking in after him silently. Preston and Brett sort of hovered awkwardly at the doorway for a bit before Preston took the initiative and found a spot to lean against the wall in the vague outline of the circle that had formed on the porch. Brett stood next to him. "Am I the designated driver again?"

"Eh, don't worry about it. Let's just cut loose tonight, cool?"

"Yeah, yeah, cool, cut loose. I think see some people dropping acid in there, so, uh… Yeah, I'll see you later."

"Later, man."

"I can drive on acid if we need to make a quick escape, by the way."

"No, you can't."

"I have done it before and I will do it again."

As he watched Brett disappear inside the bungalow, someone nudged Preston on his arm. He looked down towards the nudge to a see a guy in a beanie with gauges in his ears holding a blunt in his outstretched hand. Preston took it in his fingers. It had been maybe six months since he had done anything other than drinking, but the long hit he took came like muscle memory. He took two puffs then passed it on.

As he did so, Preston caught the denouement of the circle's conversation. One guy across the circle in a shawl neck sweater that looked impossibly comfortable was staring through the bungalow at some distant horizon as he spoke. "And then she was like, 'Whose mans is this?'... But I was like, 'Who-... Whom-... Whomst's mans am I?' You know?" He broke his thousand-yard stare to entreat his peers' thoughts.

"Word," another member of the group offered.

The blunt had gone around the circle a few times before Preston began to realize the gravity of the terrible mistake that he had made.

Shit, he thought. Was that laced or something? The fuck was happening? Was he dying? Okay, okay, just be cool. Everyone else was handling it fine. Shit, he thought again, I am going to be indisposed for quite a while. Just act cool. Oh shit, it's coming around again. Well, they're all looking at you now, just take a hit. A little one. Shit, that was a big one. Okay, you're fine, you're fine, you're not dying. Just act normal.

It was at this moment that he realized he was sort of holding his right hand up in the air as if the blunt were still between his fingers. Why was he doing that? That's not normal, put your hand down. He thrust his hands down, both balled into fists, one resting on his hip and the other arm stiff and shot straight down. Not like that, that's even weirder. Why are you standing like that? That's not how people stand. Just lean against the wall. No, just do it casually. How long have I been staring at that guy? Too long, look at that guy for a bit. He's the one talking. What are they talking about? What am I talking about? Why am I ranking Kanye albums right now, is that what we were talking about before? Is *College Dropout* better than *Dark Twisted Fantasy*? Doesn't matter, just act normal. Is your face normal? Probably. Shit, it's coming around again. I don't want it. Could I just fake it? No, they'll be able to tell, shit. Just say no thank you. No thank you. No thank you. All you have to is say no thank you, you stupid fuckface.

The guy with the gauges once more nudged his elbow and extended a hand with the blunt wrapped between his fingers. Preston opened his mouth, but then he realized that tongues are really weird, like some kind of weird tentacle thing in his mouth, and he decided that he didn't want it to move, so he didn't say anything. Shit, what's the exit strategy? Can I just leave? Is that an option? Go for it.

Preston then began backing up slowly, and promptly bumped into the wall of the bungalow, which he took as an opportunity to gracefully pivot and walk forward into the house. Stupid fuckface. What are you doing, dumbass? He must've been just standing there in the middle of the foyer for some time. Where was Brett? Where am I? He had kind of floated into what appeared to be the kitchen, without really realizing it. Now he was in a hallway. Each room in the house was lit only by one or a few small lamps and ropes of light wrapped around banisters and counters or hanging from the ceiling. It was nice, Preston thought, gave the place a certain ambience.

He was at the end of a hall, looking at a painting of sailboat hanging on a wall, next to a poem that he tried and failed to summon the attention span to read several times. The first line said "I have studied many times" but after that words just kinda stopped being real, there was something about marble or a boat or something. Suddenly, he felt a tap on his shoulder. When he turned around and looked downward slightly he saw Erin looking up at his face. She was the quiet one. What did she want? He was simply glad it wasn't Cal, as Preston still hadn't recovered from mistaking him for his brother. He doesn't even really look like my brother, but there's just something so goddamn familiar about him. It freaked Preston out. "Hi," Preston managed to say, or at least he thought he did, staring blankly down at her face. She grabbed him by the hand and led him back the other way down the hall.

Preston didn't really remember the beginning of the conversation. He just kind of blinked and he was in another room, sitting on a cracked leather couch. Erin was sitting across from him, leaning forward in a chair, so close that their legs were brushing up against each other. There was a coffee table just beside them, topped with just about everything other than coffee: bottles, tabs, pills. He had an empty glass in his hand. What did you drink? How many did you have? "I'm just stupid- I'm, I'm a piece of shit," the words were just stumbling out of Preston's mouth. He knew they were the answer even if he didn't remember the question. "That's- that's me. I'm fucking broken."

"I don't believe in broken," Erin shook her head. Her voice was soft, melodic, it made everything she said seem like perfect sense. "That's a fucking trap."

"I can't stop fucking up. That's me. And I don't get why it's so easy for everyone else to just live-"

"No, no," she shook her head again. "You can stop. You can. And no, it's not easy for people like us. But you can. People don't break, not really. Problem is, you're so afraid of failure that you don't even wanna try. So, you tell yourself that you're broken. That you're a stupid fuckface and that's just how it is, that's just who you are. That you can't change. That you're... unlovable. Because that way, you can just wallow in your fucking self-pity and you have an excuse to never try and change anything. And then you keep being shitty, and... the cycle continues. Learned fucking helplessness. People don't break, they just bend. Trust me, I've been there."

"It's easy for you to say, but She's dead," Preston snarled.

"Who?"

"She's dead and it broke me."

"You can't break, fuckface."

"I can't break?"

163

"Not if you don't want to."

"Why'd you say that word?" Preston asked.

"What?"

"Fuckface, why'd you say fuckface?"

"I didn't say fuckface."

You sound just like Her, Preston wanted to say but it died in his throat.

There must have been another gap in Preston's consciousness. When he came to again, Erin was still staring him down. "When was the last time you did something? Really did something?"

"Well I did kinda drop everything to drive across the country for a woman I've never met in person."

She started laughing. He hadn't seen her so much as smile the whole night and now she was laughing. It seemed like hours passed with her just laughing there. "That's pretty good," she said once she began to recover. "That's pretty good. That's the kinda shit you need." She was staring at him. There was something real freaky about her eyes, like she was looking down at her prey. "What do you want, Preston?" she asked.

Preston shrugged. "I'm good."

"No," she snickered. "No, I mean like- like, what do you want out of life? What do you want to be?"

I don't know. Shit, I don't know.

Preston just remained silent for what felt like a second.

"Are you alone?"

I don't know.

"Gotta be, doing what you're doing."

I guess so.

"You don't gotta be, though."

Really?

"You don't gotta be anything." She leaned out of her seat to reach something on the table. Preston watched as she put a tab of acid under her tongue. "You can be whatever you wanna be." She got up out of her seat and moved closer to Preston and sat on his lap. He couldn't feel his limbs anymore. Fuck, she was hot, wasn't she? Her eyes, he didn't break his gaze into her grey fucking eyes and he opened his mouth at her command. She put a tab on his tongue and he slid it around in his mouth, letting it settle underneath. The metallic, electric taste was something he had almost forgotten about and it came like a pang of childhood nostalgia. Erin's fingers brushed his lips on their way out. Erin. She was really hot. "You just gotta do something about it," she concluded. Would that be cheating?

She collapsed back onto the rest of the couch besides him, the ends of her legs still draped over his lap.

Cheating on who, dumbass? The dead girlfriend or the one you don't even know?

He didn't even know her.

What the hell am I doing here? This is insane. Jesus Christ, I'm fucking everything up. Again. I need to go, I can't be here anymore, I can't be this, I need to go back.

Erin stopped him before he even realized he was speaking out loud and trying to get up. How long have we been sitting here? I need to go, I have to go back. Just sit down, Preston. You're doing the right thing. There is no have to. You're

responsible for your own shit, that's it. You can't
control and you can't be controlled. She's right.
She's fucking right. God, that's even worse
though, isn't it? I'd rather go back to being totally
fucking helpless now it all comes back to me, I'm
the only one messing my life up. No, stop it stop
it stop fucking wallowing in self-pity, what good is
that? You're gonna have a bad trip if you keep
thinking about shit like that. Think about literally
anything else. Think about anything other than
yourself, just for once you miserable piece of shit.
How long have I been here? I don't think I'm
tripping yet, not really. It is worse though, definitely. I'm not an adult. Maybe I can be, people
don't break. I can't break. I should be an adult,
I'm twenty-one fucking years old but I'm not really. When did we leave Vermont? I can't even
drive a stick. I don't have a firm grasp on what a
401k is. I haven't seen *Casablanca*. I'm not an
adult, what makes me qualified to run my life?
What the fuck am I doing here? I don't even
know her and I'm just driving across the country
to see her I don't even know what my end game
here is. I'm not a real person. Is there supposed to
be some kinda happy ending to all this? I need to
get away but the faster I go the harder I crash.
How long have I been here? I need to leave.
Where am I? Preston was about to reach for his
phone but then he couldn't feel his fingers and
spent quite a while thinking about the fact that,
like, he can think about moving his arm without
actually moving it, which is really fucking weird
when you, like, think about it, you know? No,
stop it, I have to go back. What if I die here? Am

I dying? I can't break but I can definitely die. She died. This is how She died. I have to go back to Vermont before I fuck everything up more than I already have. Where's Brett where's the Civic? Erin was on top of him again shushing him. Preston, if all you're gonna do is go back to Vermont, go back to just being a helpless piece of shit in your comfortable misery,
it will never get better.
You will never get better.
You might as well kill yourself.
You might as well take every fucking pill in this house and
die here on this couch.
It will never get better.
You
will never get better.
Unless you keep going. That's what you have to do. kill myself. You have to keep fucking going and never look back. All gas, don't brake for shit. never get better. Never look back it's all just weighing you down, just hit the gas. die here. Come on, we're gonna hit the Strip. all gas no brake people don't brake. Preston was floating through the bungalow never better. Preston was in the back of the minivan Erin was next to him she was holding his hand all gas don't break Cal was driving Brett was halfway out the window singing some shit with a bottle in his hand. Have I met Cal before why is he so goddamn familiar kill myself. They got gelato on the strip? Brett was asking. Cal and Erin were laughing at something they have the same laugh maybe they're twins after all never better. There were cars all gas don't

brake and buildings fucking everywhere lights
fucking everywhere i can't brake streetlights headlights neon a lighter lights lights lights lights
   Black.

2

Preston had blacked out more times than he would care to admit in his life, and thus far he had always woken up from them in one piece. Give or take. He had always found that, as he woke up and stretched his brittle muscles and aching bones, he was at least instantly able to tell that time had passed in some capacity. How much time had passed, and what had occurred during that time, was a mystery and attempting to solve that mystery sheerly through mental efforts to recollect was about as futile as attempting to explain color to a blind man, whom is also deaf, quadriplegic, hostile to new ideas, and all around a bit of a dick. His past blackouts had all occurred in Vermont, and thus when he awoke, he would find himself at his apartment or his dorm before that or his parent's house before that, and on one occasion, in the middle of his 8:30 Economics of Globalization lecture. So, his current situation, arising in a room entirely foreign to him, was somewhat novel.

He was lying in a room.

On a bed.

It was a bedroom, presumably.

He might have been able to divine more, but his head was currently on its side, half burrowed in a pillow that smelled ambiguous, staring at drywall mere inches away, and he was thoroughly reluctant to stir any part of his body. When he eventually did manage to roll over onto his other side, his body grumbling at him with pain, he found himself facing a window on the opposite wall. Out the window, past some curtains with a trippy floral sequence and a string of lights, he could see the minivan, parked mostly on the road and slightly on the sidewalk. The bungalow. He was at the bungalow. And, judging from the light outside, it was either the evening or early in the morning.

He lay on that side a little longer then flopped onto his back. After staring at the ceiling for a moment, he looked down. He was wearing a suit. A nice suit, too. A suit that probably costed more than the Civic, from the looks of it. It had a purple silk neck tie that was currently untied and wrapped around his neck like a scarf. Preston wondered if he had ever worn anything purple before this very moment. A moment longer, just laying there, swimming in his head. The first things he was able to move were his arms. He thrust his hands into the suit's pockets.

Keys.

Wallet.

A few things he couldn't identify by his finger-tips alone.

When he brought his hand out of his right pocket, he was holding a disorganized wad of cash, and a few casino chips held loosely between them. A lot of fucking cash. A weirdly large amount of cash.

Satisfied with the quantity of weirdly large, Preston shoved the wad back in his pocket without counting it. He dug in his pocket further. Phone. He needed his phone.

Keys.

Wallet.

A napkin with a phone number written on it and some chewed up gum spat into it.

A guitar pick. Preston had never owned nor played a guitar, at least so far as he could remember.

A few nuts and bolts. Something, somewhere out there was currently structurally unsound.

No phone. He shot up into a sitting position and surveyed the room around him. It was mostly bare aside from the bed, a desk without a chair, and decorations that were copious and lacking in any consistent theme. He finally exhaled when he saw that his phone was on the desk, charging. He summoned the strength to get up off the bed and amble over to the desk.

4:28 PM. Friday, December 22nd. So, he had missed two nights and a day. Slightly alarming, but he had gone longer. Two missed calls. One from his mom. One from Dalia. One new voicemail.

He dialed his voicemail and leaned against the desk. "One. New. Message. December. 21st." A long beep.

"Hello, Preston, it's Dalia." She didn't have to say her name; her voice was more than enough. But he was glad to hear it for some reason. "Just getting back to you since I missed your last call. Sorry about that. But, from the voicemail it sounds like you're having a good time. That's college, I guess, huh? Anyways, stay safe. We'll talk later." The voicemail abruptly cut after that promise.

"One. Saved. Message," a robotic female voice announced. "June. Twenty fifth." A long beep as he felt his stomach churning.

"Hey there," She said, Her voice light and playful, Her cadence bouncy. "Call me back, fuckface."

He hung up the phone and stuffed it in his pocket, then just sat there for a moment, not quite sure how to proceed. Brett was the next priority, he supposed. Preston got up, and slowly wandered through the bungalow a bit, not quite remembering the layout of the place. He ended up in the kitchen somehow, where Cal was sitting at the island table over a bowl of Froot Loops. Cal smiled. "Hey there," he said. "It's the fucking lizard man."

"Right on," Preston said slowly.

Cal scoffed. "You're sober, aren't you?"

"It would appear so."

"And you don't remember shit."

"Two for two."

Cal let out a deep laugh from his Froot Loop laden belly. "I like you," he said, pointing his milky spoon at Preston. "Even when you're sober."

"Thanks, man," Preston mumbled. "Hey, can I ask you something?"

Cal sighed. "No, we've never met before you came here." He took another mouthful of Froot Loops. "You kept asking me while you were fucked up."

"Huh," Preston said. "You just remind me of someone I guess… What's with the suit, by the way?"

Again, Cal scoffed. "I don't know, you wanted it."

"Really?"

"Yeah, you were pretty fucking insistent on it too."

"Weird. I don't even know how to tie a tie."

"Evidently," Preston heard Erin's voice behind him. He turned to catch a glimpse of her striding down the hall.

He turned back to Cal. "Where's Brett?"

Cal stared at him blankly. "He wasn't in there with you?"

"Nah, man."

"He passed out too. We left him in there. Huh. You seen him, Erin?"

"Yeah," she called out from some distant corner of the bungalow.

"Where is he?"

"He left."

"Shit, did he take the Civic?" Preston asked, looking out the open door.

"Yeah," Erin's voice confirmed.

"Well, do you know where he went?"

"Nah," Erin answered.

"What's the last thing you remember him saying?" Cal asked.

"Man, I barely remember fucking Thurs-" Preston stopped abruptly. "I think I know where to find him," he announced. "Can I borrow the van?"

"Sure," Cal said. Then suddenly, "Oh shit." He put down his spoon and got up, disregarding the Froot Loops. "Almost forgot." He strode over to one of the kitchen cabinets and reached in. He pulled out a plastic grocery bag and tossed it on the table. "Your winnings. Figured I'd hold onto 'em for you until you sobered up. I promise it's all there."

Preston took a few cautious steps towards the table and peeked inside the bag. He saw precisely one metric shit ton of dollar bills. Some were tied in little rolls with rubber bands, others just loosely floating, some slightly damp for some reason. As far as Preston could see, there was nothing small-er than a twenty-dollar bill. "Uh..." Preston be-gan. "How- uh... How did- How did this hap-pen?"

"What do you mean?"

"I- What- Did I-" Preston stammered. "What goods or services did I exchange for this money?"

Cal smiled. "You're in Vegas, man. You won it, fair and square. More or less."

3

Night had fallen on Vegas again, and with it a cool, pleasant breeze prowled the city streets alongside the minivan. The van tumbled down the roads, its ponderous body and rickety skeleton letting out a symphony of screeches and murmurs with every movement. The brakes were concerningly ineffective. Preston dared not mush the beast beyond a slow crawl for the whole ride, his gaze glancing between the road and the GPS on his phone below. There were precisely four moments in particular on the fifteen-minute ride where Preston was sure that he had entered a situation which could only end in car wreck and death; however, there were no casualties by the time he pulled into the parking lot in front of a small stand on a street corner. On top of the stand, in ostentatious neon cursive letters befitting its proximity to the Strip, was written "Giuseppe's."

The stand was relatively empty of people and full of that tragic air about a small business that is struggling to continue its existence. There was, however, one figure seated at one of the outdoor picnic tables, a small bowl before him. Preston got out of the van and walked up to the stand.

"Brett," he called out to the figure, but the figure didn't turn around. It was definitely Brett, Preston approached from the side and could see his scraggly brown beard, his thick glasses, his curly mop of tawny hair. "Hey, Brett," Preston said as came up to the table. This time Brett couldn't resist flicking his eyes towards him, but instantly turned back to the bowl in front of him without speaking. "What's up, man?" Preston gave him a friendly tap on the shoulder.

Still, no response. "Whatcha doing?" Preston asked.

Brett swallowed another mouthful of his food. "I may not have friends, but I do have gelato," he mumbled without looking up at Preston.

"What the hell are you talking about, man?"

"What are you doing here, anyway?" Brett asked.

Preston paused, befuddled. "It's- We gotta get going, man. Come on, we gotta get to Anaheim."

"You mean L.A."

"Your uncle's in Anaheim, man."

This time Brett looked up at his face, a certain soft sorrow in his eyes. "You don't remember, do you?"

"Last thing I remember is Thursday night."

"You told me everything, dude."

"What do you mean?"

"Well, after you gambled all of my fucking money, you told me what all this was. The phone calls, the book, L.A., Dalia, everything, dude. You even called her."

Preston was silent.

"Well?" Brett said. "You gonna say anything?"

Preston rubbed his brow. "I don't know what you want me to say."

Brett stabbed his gelato with his spoon. "How about 'Sorry?' How about 'Sorry for lying to you and manipulating you and dragging you on this crazy fucking goose chase-'"

"Brett, I didn't mean-"

"And 'I'm sorry for being a shitty friend and just being mean all the time and taking everything that happens out on you, cause you're an easy target-'"

"Brett-" Preston's voice took an edge.

"'And for gambling all the fucking money your mom gave you-'"

"Okay, you want the fucking money? The money's your goddamn problem?" Preston shouted, then stormed off back to the van. He flung open the back door and grabbed the grocery bag, then marched back to the picnic table.

"Preston-"

"No, no, you want the fucking money? Here's the fucking money," Preston said, slamming wads of bills down on the table.

"Dude-"

"No, no, it's no trouble. Here, two thousand one hundred fourteen fucking dollars and sixty-four fucking cents. Keep the change."

"I don't care about the money, Preston," Brett shouted. "I- I care about you."

"Oh yeah, you care about your shitty friend."

"I-"

"Who's been an asshole ever since his girlfriend died."

"I shouldn't have-"

"Yeah, but you did."

"I didn't mean it like that."

"Yes, yes you did. You meant it exactly like that. You're probably right too, just fucking admit it, say what you were gonna say."

Brett was silent for a second. "It's... weird that we never talked about it."

"Oh, I'm so sorry I didn't want to talk about my dead girlfriend, how rude of me."

"We've been best friends for years. I was there for you. I tried to help. But you didn't say a word about it to me, you just kept drinking and pushing everyone away. And now, you're pouring it all out to this woman you don't even know, and you're driving across the country to find her, and you're lying to me and manipulating me so I'll come along with you like some kind of sidekick, how do you think that makes me feel?"

"I don't know what I'm doing," Preston shouted, shrugging his arms. "Is that what you want to hear? I have no fucking idea what I'm doing." He ran a trembling hand through his hair and sniffled. "I don't know what the... correct procedure is when your fucking girlfriend kills Herself. No clue. But I'm doing something. I need to do something. All my life, even before Her, I haven't done shit, I've just been along for the ride and I can't fucking take it anymore. If you care about me-"

"I do care about you. That's why I can't keep watching you destroy yourself over and over. I want you to get better. I want to help you, but I have no fucking clue either. And I can't do this anymore. I can't keep enabling you, I can't sit here and watch you do this to yourself."

Preston stared down at him. "What are you saying?"

"I… think it'd be best if we parted ways now."

"I don't understand."

"You don't need me. Or maybe you do, I don't know anymore, but you sure as hell aren't acting like you do."

"Brett, I-" Preston scoffed in disbelief. "You can't just… go like that."

"I'm-"

"You're my friend-"

"And I'll always be your friend, but-"

"You can't just drop out of this."

"Out of what?" Preston was silent. "Out of *your* story?" Brett sighed. "Look, I- I know you've had a lot of shitty stuff happen to you," he said softly. "I know you deserve better than that. But… I'm trying so hard. And it's taken so much out of me. And I think, what I've learned is… You can't fix anyone else. And you know I'd do fucking anything for you. I'll be there for you when you want to get better, but I can't help you until you do."

"Well then, you better go home." The words just came out of Preston's mouth.

The gelato stand was silent for a moment, the storm ended, the battle over, the gunfire ceased. Brett let out another heavy sigh. "Yeah…" He dug in his pocket and put the Civic's keys on the table. "I'm gonna stay with Cal and Erin tonight. I called Uncle Quade, he's gonna come get me tomorrow. Take the Civic." Brett looked him in the eyes. "You know how to find me if you need to. But I hope you can be happy, dude… Whatever you're looking for in L.A., I hope you find it."

Preston paused. "Brett, I'm-"

"Don't. Let's just… shut the fuck up for once."

Preston lingered for a moment, before he grabbed the bag and the keys. He wanted to say something else, but he didn't know what.

So, he left.

California

1

Preston turned the key in the ignition. The low hum and high rattle of the Civic's engine was abruptly cut off, leaving room for silence and the tapping of rain hitting the windshield and the roof. He let the wipers come to a halt, and it wasn't long before the cityscape before him was hidden behind wavy, translucent curtains of water. The city lights were amplified and scattered about the warped horizon. The sky was pitch black, the moon and the few stars that were visible in the L.A. sky covered up with murky clouds. He was pulled over at the side of Mulholland Drive, and all that he could see of the road was the headlights of cars whizzing by him every few minutes. He simply sat there for a moment, watching L.A. shifting behind the rain. Then, he slid a hand into the pocket of his hoodie and pulled out his phone. He opened his messaging app. Dalia was the first name on the list, and the only one he had talked to in God knows how long. "can you talk?" he sent.

Waiting.

The four minutes between messages felt like an hour. "It would be my pleasure" she replied. He was still grinning as her name came up on the screen and he accepted the call.

"Hey," he said into the receiver.

"Hey yourself."

"What's up?"

"You tell me," she laughed softly. "You wanted to talk."

What's up is I'm in L.A., he thought about saying. Instead, he went with, "Nothing much."

She laughed again. "Well, thanks for the update."

"I just, uh… I just wanted to hear your voice, I guess."

"Well, here I am in all my glory."

"Oh, thank you, thank you, your highness."

After the chuckles had faded, there was nothing for a moment. Just the two of them listening to the melody of each other breathing into the receivers. Dalia spoke up after some time. "So," she began. "What do you want to talk about?"

"I don't know," Preston sighed. He lowered his seat and lay down, replacing the L.A. skyline with the headliner of the Civic's interior, then let his eyelids droop closed to the thin crackle of the phone. "How's the erotica business?"

"Oh," she sighed too. "Not bad. Doing more promotion and marketing bullshit than writing at this point, though."

"For *Sexting*?"

"Yeah. That's what I get for self-publishing it. But hey, it's doing decent numbers, so I can't really complain. Well, I can, and I probably will, but not right now, at least."

"You know, I can't believe that I haven't asked you this yet, but what made you want to write erotica?"

"What, aside from the kink of it?" she laughed.

"Hey, man, I'm not judging, I'm just curious."

"Well, to be perfectly honest, I don't really consider what I do erotica myself."

"No?"

"No."

"I'd be fascinated to see your idea of what is, then."

"I mean there is sex, obviously-"

"A fair amount of it."

"Right, but... That's not the point of it. It's never just about the sex. It's more... more about the romance of it, for me. Just two people making each other feel less lonely. That's what I was always drawn to. Sex is just the most primal, powerful symbol of that that we have."

"You know, I wouldn't have pegged you for a romantic type when I first met you."

"Maybe that's because when we first spoke I was threatening to call the cops on you."

"Yeah, yeah, that'll do it." Another moment, another silence that Preston could feel himself melting into. "You, uh..." he began. "You..."

"Take your time," she scoffed.

"You dated a lot?"

"Uh, yeah, yeah I did. More so back in the day. When *I* was in college I couldn't stay single for ten minutes. Had a new boyfriend every other week. A girlfriend or two thrown in there as well."

"Really?"

"Yes."

"Right on, right on."

"What about you?"

"Hmm, me? No, just- no, uh, just the one. And now you, of course."

"Of course," she grinned. They exchanged a few words silently. "How's Vermont?" Dalia eventually asked out loud.

"Uh..." Preston began. "You know, Vermont, uh… Vermont's Vermont."

"Yes, Vermont is indeed Vermont."

"How's L.A.?" Preston asked as he looked down over the city.

"Oh, you know, it's Los Angeles," Dalia teased.

"Does it ever snow in L.A.?"

"No, not really."

Preston thought that he might miss the winters, at least a little. "You've lived there all your life, right?"

"Yes, born and raised."

"You ever thought about going somewhere else?"

"I mean, we all have fantasies, but not seriously, no. Everything I wanted was here. The music industry, then my publishing company…"

"Oh shit," Preston exclaimed, his eyes shooting open.

"What?"

"I totally fucking forgot."

"What?" Dalia repeated.

"You promised to sing for me."

"Oh, god."

"A promise is a promise, Dalia Peterson."

"What would I even sing for you?"

"I don't know, whatever, uh... whatever you're feeling, you know?"

She was silent for a few seconds. "I could do 'Auld Lang Syne.'"

"'Auld Lang Syne?'" he chuckled.

"Yeah, you know, the New Year's song."

"I know, I know, that's just- I wasn't expecting that at all. You know, it's closer to Christmas than it is New Year's."

"Well, yeah, but Christmas wasn't such a big deal for me growing up."

"Really?"

"Yeah, we never had money for gifts, we weren't religious at all."

"That sucks."

"It didn't bother me much. I didn't know what Christmas was supposed to be. Didn't see what all the fuss was about. I was always much more excited for New Year's. I got to stay up late, our landlord would let us get on the roof of our apartment building to watch the fireworks," she spoke softly into the phone, as if telling a secret. "We had 'Auld Lang Syne' sung by Guy Lombardo on vinyl, and my mom would break out her mom's record player every year. It was the closest thing we had to a family heirloom. Then, one year it broke, so my mom went out and bought me a walkman and a cd of 'Auld Lang Syne.' That was pretty much the only Christmas present I ever got. I just always liked the idea of New Year's too. It's like a fresh start, or something. There's some hope in it."

"Well, now you've just got me all hyped to hear it."

"Oh, alright, alright." Preston adjusted his seat back up to look at Los Angeles while there was a hesitant pause in the call. *"Should auld acquaintance be forgot and never brought to mind?"* she began singing in a low, smoky whisper. That mixture of the faded warmth of memory and the numb, hollow pain of loss that is nostalgia was her voice as she carried on for a couple verses. Preston thought it was the best thing he had heard in a long time; she filled him with an ecstatic nausea and heart pounding serenity. *"We'll take a cup of kindness yet, for auld lang syne,"* she eventually finished, holding out the last few notes.

Preston let a little silence pass, then held the phone up to his ear with his shoulder and clapped his hands into the receiver. "Thank you, thank you," she laughed in response to the applause. "I'm taking a bow."

"That really was great."

"Thanks."

"You know," Preston began after a moment, "there was always some part of me that just wanted to drop everything and head west."

"Really?"

"Yeah, yeah. I think just about every kid in the northeast wants to at some point. California. There's just something… I don't know-"

"Romantic?"

"Romantic. Something romantic about the west."

"It's not that great, trust me. But then again, Hawaii was always my day dream."

"So, we just keep going west and everything will be fine."

"Sounds about right."

Little did they know that if you keep going west, eventually you end up where you started.

"Man, I could go for some fireworks right now." Preston said. "And some Chinese food. With all this New Year's talk, I mean."

"Well, tell you what, it is... 11:34 here, so, what, 2:34 for you? Let's make it New Year's right now. At 35, we got a fresh chance, we're living in a new year."

"That sounds nice."

"We'll do the countdown too. Just... wait for it. Five."

"Four," Preston joined her in unison.

"Three."

"Two."

"One."

2

Tap.

Preston didn't quite register the tap, and he didn't stir from his slumber at all, but he did hear it.

Another few taps.

This time, Preston's eyelids fluttered a bit and then spent another moment squinting against the garish sunshine of a blue skied morning. His eyes scanned around a bit. He was once more lying on his back, staring at the Civic's headliner. His eyes slowly wandered to the window, where a figure stood behind the thin glass screen. It was a cop, middle aged, bald, with a greying mustache and a pair of sunglasses perched on his nose. Instinctively, Preston lifted his hands up into plain sight slowly. The cop pointed a finger downwards.

Preston's throat was clenched shut. He lifted his left hand and rolled the window all the way down. He opened his mouth, but then he remembered: don't speak unless spoken to. "Good morning, sir," the cop said.

"Hello, officer," Preston managed to blurt out. He was still lying in his reclined seat, his hands placed carefully on his knees, in the cop's line of vision.

"Can you sit up for me?" the cop asked.

Preston once again slowly and deliberately lifted a hand, and then pulled his seat back to the upright position. Once more, he was looking down on L.A. He was still parked on the side of Mulholland. His hands snapped into position, glued onto the steering wheel before him. "How long have you been here?" the cop said.

"Um... Since last night, officer."

"When last night?"

"About 11:30. Sir."

"Did you have anything to drink last night?"

"No, no, sir. I just- I drove straight from Vegas-"

"Vegas, huh?"

"Yes, sir. I was... tired, so I pulled over to rest my eyes, and..."

"I see."

"I'm sorry, sir."

"And you're sure you didn't have any drinks?"

"Yes, sir."

"Any marijuana?"

"No, sir."

"No medications?"

"Yes, sir."

"Yes, you're on medications?"

"No- I- I meant-"

"I understand." The cop stared at Preston's eyes through his sunglasses, then looked back at his car for a second. He rested his hands on his belt. Preston tried not to look at his holster. "License and registration."

Preston's hands didn't leave the wheel. "Uh… license is in my front pocket, registration in the glove compartment, is that alright, sir?"

"Go ahead."

Preston reached for each of the items, making sure not deviate from the specified path in the slightest. He handed them both through the window, and the cop paced back to his car. Once Preston watched him disappear into the cruiser from his rearview mirror, he was finally able to exhale for the first time since he had awoken. He rubbed his face and closed his eyes for a brief respite. Before he could do anything else, the cop had appeared and was handing him back his papers. "Vermont plates, huh?" the cop said. "What brings you out here?"

"I'm, uh- I'm visiting a friend of mine."

"Drove the whole way?"

"Yes, sir."

"On your own?"

Preston paused. "My friend came, but uh… we parted ways back in Vegas."

"You headed into the city?"

"Yes, sir."

"Good luck with that. Probably won't get too far in by car."

Preston stared at him blankly. "Why's that, sir?"

"Riots. Been watching the news at all?"

"I, uh-… I try to avoid all that."

The cop grunted. "Probably got the right idea there. Better for your health, not worrying about all that malarkey."

Preston couldn't think of anything to say, so he simply nodded.

"Well, welcome to Los Angeles, anyway." The cop gave him one last look, then nodded. "Stay safe."

"Thank you, sir. You too."

The cop began striding away. A question occurred to Preston, and he thought about calling out after him, but instantly decided against it. Instead, he whipped out his phone and spent the next few minutes scrolling around on a map of his general vicinity. Soon enough, he found a motel just on the outskirts of the city, probably away from the war zones. Eight reviews. Two point one stars. Preston decided that this was a sufficient number of stars and kicked the Civic back to life, then got back onto the road.

It was only moments before he arrived at his destination. The Civic swerved into an empty parking lot just before a small motel, two dingy floors with all the enchanting sleaze one could expect of such an institution. The building looked like it was hastily erected over some lost summer of the Fifties, and was already dated by the time its construction finished. Preston slipped out of the car and walked into the mouth of the ancient monolith.

The motel's reception area was shaded and dim, the curtains drawn entirely shut and the only source of light a few yellowing lamps sparsely scattered throughout. There was a man behind the imposing figure of the hickory desk, leaning back in an office chair with his feet propped up on the desktop. His slicked back salt and pepper hair was unkempt, his face unshaven, his eyes shut. Preston approached the desk. "Hello?" he said.

The man didn't stir. Preston waited a moment, looking around the empty room for assistance. Then, he prodded one of the man's feet. Still, no response. He coughed passive aggressively to no effect. Finally, he saw a bell on the desk before him, and stared at it for a moment before gingerly ringing it.

The man snapped to life, his eyes opening and his body shooting to sit upright in his chair. "What do you want?" he growled.

"I, uh- I need a room."

The man looked him up and down. He pulled his chair in to the desk and grabbed a pencil and a stray piece of paper nearby. A cigarette found its way into the corner of his mouth. "Are you a moron?" he asked through the cigarette.

"I'm sorry?"

"Are you a moron? Or an imbecile, idiot, et cetera."

Preston paused. "I don't understand."

"In the technical sense." The man finally got around to lighting his cigarette. "Meaning, do you have an IQ score of below seventy?"

"I- No, no, I don't."

The man began scribbling furiously on a piece of paper. "Are you currently carrying any infectious diseases?"

"Not that I know of."

The man stopped scribbling and stared at him blankly.

"No," Preston confirmed.

The man stared a moment longer, then brought his eyes back to the paper and continued scribbling. "Do you have a criminal record?"

"I do not."

"Are you a debauchee?"

"A what?"

"A debauchee, one who engages in debauchery."

"N- No."

"Are you currently or have you ever been under the employ of the United States government?"

"Nope."

"Are you a political agitator?"

"No."

"So, you're not in Los Angeles for the protests, then."

"Right, just… on vacation."

"Very good. I'm a simple man. I value discretion in regards to my patron's personal affairs, but I do not want any trouble in my establishment."

"Understandable."

The man ceased his writing and ducked below the desk. When he came back up, he was lifting an arm, displaying a shotgun. "I intend to keep any and all trouble out of my establishment."

Preston stared at the gun with wide eyes. "Right."

"You don't have to worry about any of those protesters here."

"Wow, okay, uh, thank you."

The man stared at him silently for another brief moment, still displaying the shotgun. He didn't lower it as he used his other hand to open one of the desk's numerous drawers. His hand plunged into the drawer and after a second of jingling and jangling, returned with a key in hand.

"Room two thirteen."

"Thank you," Preston said again as he gingerly took the key.

"Get settled in, then come back here and pay for your stay." Preston nodded silently. The man didn't break his glare. "Two thirteen, eh?"

"Right."

"Two," the man said, writing again. "Thirteen," he finished, then looked back up at Preston. "You let me know if there's any trouble, now."

"Will do," Preston said, beginning to slowly back out of the room.

"Two thirteen."

"Two thirteen," Preston confirmed as he hurried out the door way.

He shut the door behind him and stood still there in the California sun for a moment. He sighed and pressed on, journeying into the maze of rooms to find his own. When he arrived at room two thirteen, he opened the door to find a chamber of grime. A window with a sweeping view of the neighboring building's brick wall. A speckled mirror above a wooden, vaguely sticky vanity. Rumpled, yellowing sheets on a bed that was almost made.

This would do.

For the time being, at least, until he could meet Dalia. Perhaps that would only be one night. Perhaps it wouldn't even be that long.

3

Jacket, vest, tie. Too much.

Jacket, vest. No, what the hell was that?

Just the vest? No. Just no.

Just the jacket? Warmer.

Jacket, tie. That one's alright too.

Preston thought that he might need a new tie, though. Purple just wasn't his color, he had decided. On top of that was the fact that there were already several small, unidentifiable stains on the silk that gave him some bad vibes. For a moment, he stared at his own face in the speckled glass of his motel mirror. He scratched his chin. Should he shave? No, she liked the beard, he thought. Definitely not shaving.

Days had passed. Several of them.

Days that mostly consisted of sleeping and driving around the city aimlessly. A few of the afternoons had been spent examining the aftermath of the protests. Shattered windows, discarded signs and other garbage littering the ground, police dressed like soldiers patrolling the streets. The protests themselves had seemingly died down by the time Preston got the chance to examine them, but he still managed to catch glimpses of marching masses and hear echoes of chants and songs, of the name Lavar Gray. He had felt like a civilian caught in the crossfire of a revolution, but some force of gravity made him continue to orbit the war zone. Death felt close in the city. It also felt close as he attempted to avoid the motel's owner and his shotgun and his hawkish eyes every time he ventured out of the room. However, he was never doing anything in particular in these days, just violently murdering time until he had the courage to take his next step.

As it turned out, he found it in a bottle of vodka that he was keeping in the drawer of the nightstand next to his bed. He sat down on the bed, and stared out his window, squarely into the brick wall painted with strokes of orange and pink by the setting of the sun. He got the bottle out of the drawer and took a quick swig. His phone was laying on the top of the night stand, clear of any notifications, waiting for him. He stared at it for a while, then took it in his palms.

He raised it to his ear and listened to it ring.

Once.

Twice.

Three times. He rose to his feet and paced the narrow room.

Four.

He meandered over to face the mirror once more and had just about given up hope when the fifth ring began, but it was abruptly cut off and replaced with the crackle of another line. Silence. Words didn't come. His mouth was slightly agape, his lips just parted, and he could neither open nor close it fully. "Preston?" Dalia's voice appeared in his ear.

"What are you doing tonight?" He watched the words tumbling out of his lips in the mirror.

"What?"

"Tonight, do you have any plans?" There was something surreal in watching his own face move.

"No... Why do you ask?"

"I, uh..." He had rehearsed the moment a million times over and over and over in his head. He wasn't stumbling over his words; the pause was a planned affectation in order to sound natural. He had decided to play it cool, to act like there was nothing surprising in his presence in L.A. or they're getting together, like that was the only logical end of their story. "I was wondering if you'd want to go on a date with me."

Dalia paused. "I don't understand, Preston."

"Well, I'm- I'm in town, and I'd like to see you."

"What do you mean?" she asked.

"I- I mean... I want to see you."

"Preston... I don't-" she let out a huff of breath into the receiver. "I don't understand. You're in L.A.?"

"Y- Yeah."

"How- Why...?" Silence. "What are you doing here?"

"I'm," his voice trailed off. He didn't have an answer. All this time and he never thought of an answer to that question.

"You didn't come all the way here for me, did you?"

Preston answered silently. He had to turn away from the blank stare in the mirror, the face that couldn't answer the fucking question.

"Jesus Christ," she sighed again. "You understand how fucking insane that is, don't you?"

"Dalia, I'm… I'm so fucking tired of everything. I'm tired of being alone, and I know that you are too. I need to change something-"

"So, what you just expect that you can show up at my doorstep and all your problems will be magically solved?"

"No, I just-" he was pacing the shag carpet of the motel room. "I want to be with you. I thought this is what you wanted too."

"You need to leave."

"You said you wanted to be with me."

"I don't-"

"You said it."

"I shouldn't have."

"But you meant it."

"I don't know. I don't know why I said it." Preston could hear her voice cracking. His own throat was clenching shut as he began to feel tears forming in his eyes. "I can't do this, Preston."

"Dalia. I- I don't understand. You said that you wanted me."

"I shouldn't have said that."

"Did I ever mean anything to you?"

"Oh god, now you're starting on this again."

"Just answer the question, Dalia."

"It's complicated, Preston."

"Dalia-"

"My name isn't Dalia," she suddenly interjected.

"What?"

"It's a fucking pen name. My name is Madison. I'm not Dalia Peterson, I'm Madison fucking Brown."

Preston paused. "Okay, well…"

"You don't get it. I don't know you, Preston. You don't know me. You don't even know my fucking name."

"Well, that doesn't matter."

"Of course it matters."

"No, it doesn't."

"You've never seen my face, you've never been in the same state as me until now-"

"That doesn't matter. I know you. I poured my fucking heart out to you-"

"But this isn't real, Preston."

"You know me better than anyone, I poured my fucking heart-"

"Preston-"

"And I know you."

"You don't know the first fucking thing about me."

"I know this is what you want. On some level, you need this just as much as I do-"

"I'm married, Preston."

Preston couldn't find anything to say. For the moment, those three words were the only thing ricocheting in his mind. "What?" eventually escaped his throat.

"I'm married. Happily fucking married. I live in a fucking house in the fucking suburbs and sleep in a bed with my fucking husband every night."

"Well, if you're so happy, what the hell are you doing talking to me?"

"What?" it was her turn to ask now.

"How would your fucking husband like to know that you've been cheating on him-"

"I *never* cheated."

"Oh, come on."

"I've never met you."

"Even you know that's bullshit."

"It didn't mean anything, Preston. Is that what you need to hear to get this through your fucking head? It didn't mean anything. Never. We were two people trying to be a little less lonely. That's all it ever was. I do not love you. I don't know you, and you need to go home."

He shook his head, as if she was there, as if she could see. At some point he had lowered down to sit on the floor, his back against the wall below the window. "I don't believe you. You're just scared-"

"Scared of what?" she shouted.

"Scared of doing anything real with your life. I was too, but this-"

"I've done plenty. I have a husband, I wrote books, I live in L.A., that's what's real."

"You don't care about any of that. That's not enough for you-"

"Just because your life is fucking miserable doesn't mean everyone else's is."

"Happy people don't say the shit you said to me."

He heard a lo-fi slamming on the other side of the line, something like a fist crashing down. "You need to leave."

"I can't."

"I don't want to talk to you anymore."

"Dalia, please-"

"That's not my fucking name."
The call ended.

4

On the other side of the glass bulwark of the Civic's windshield was the rolling azure hills of the Pacific receding into the horizon, with a modest pier stretching out just barely past the border between the beach and the sea. It was a pleasant enough afternoon, the sun perched up in a clear sky. California winter was practically Vermont summer. There was a crowd just short of a mob populating the pier and scattered around the beach below, all of its members seemingly just wandering about aimlessly in groups of twos and threes and fours. The city seemed just shy of being at war with itself not a week earlier, and now these people had nothing in the world to worry about besides their company. The Civic was resting on an asphalt parking lot just before the sands. "Okay, so now you're gonna want to take the fat end and sort of fold it up like this, and then you're gonna feed it through that loop you create and pull through. Make sure you get a nice knot on that," a voice echoed throughout the car. "Then, just pull the skinny end until you've got it tight enough and… Voila!"

Preston had never seen the Pacific before that morning, but by now he had taken his eyes off of it. Instead, his gaze was alternating between his phone, laying on its side and propped up on the windshield, and the length of silk around his neck. He had replaced the purple tie he got in Vegas with a more spartan and elegant black tie, though now he was having a few seconds thoughts. He looked like he was going to a funeral. On the phone's screen was a man's torso and arms draped in a slightly oversized dress shirt and a freshly tied tie. Preston had managed to craft a decent enough knot out of his own tie, but the skinny end comically outstretched the fat end when he pulled it up to his neck. "Okay guys, thanks for watching, hope it was helpful. Don't forget to smash that motherfucking like button and hit subscribe if you-"

Preston picked up his phone and closed the video, then tossed it aside onto the passenger seat. It took a few more goes before he had successfully tied both a presentable knot and a properly lengthed tie. Once he was satisfied with his handiwork, he took a deep breath. And he sat. And he watched the waves. His fingers were shaking until he started the Civic and gripped the steering wheel with white knuckles.

It was only a few suspenseful minutes before he reached his destination, carefully navigating the streets of Santa Monica and obsessively referring to his phone for directions. It led him into a nice enough neighborhood, slightly too urban to be suburban, but certainly affluent and probably gentrified. The Civic pulled over to the side of the street in front of a house that perfectly embodied the unassuming decadence of the vaguely upper middle or perhaps lower upper class, right down to the Mercedes in the driveway and the in-ground pool in the back.

"You have arrived at your destination," his phone declared.

And then he just sat there. A moment passed. He pulled the key out of the ignition. He checked his tie and donned his jacket. He looked at his phone one last time before tossing it aside onto the passenger seat and getting out of the car. It all still felt surreal. He could hardly believe that he had made it this far, that he had driven as far west as west goes, that he was walking up a California walkway up to the door of a California house with the California sun blanketing him. It was so god-damn hot. His heart was climbing further up his throat and pounding harder with every step to-wards the door.

Then he was standing on the porch.

He was there.

It took him another moment, silent aside from the ambient chatter of a city, to work up the gall to reach out and tap his knuckles on the door. In what seemed like mere seconds, the door swung open.

And she was there.

There was something surprising about her, and Preston couldn't quite pin down its exact source. She was as she had described. She had brunette hair chopped at her collarbones, a bit lighter than he had pictured. Her figure was a bit slim beneath her high waisted jeans and the slightly oversized button up she had tucked into them and she stood nearly as tall as him across the threshold of her home. Maybe early thirties, Preston figured. There was no one outstanding feature that was amiss, and yet there was some ineffable disconnect between the voice that had called out from his phone and written across his screen and the woman standing before him now. Maybe it was merely the fact that she was there, existing as a corporeal being. That she was real at all. For a moment, her big, sunken grey eyes merely scanned him up and down. Her heart shaped face sunk deeper into the scowl it had already been wearing before she turned, leaving the door open and calling behind her, "Come in, Preston."

She had already disappeared into the bowels of the house by the time he had worked up the will to set foot inside and head down the entryway corridor. His gaze crawled all up and down the house, the furniture that was sleek and modern yet tinged with nostalgia for the classics, the vaguely impressionist art dangling on the sterile white walls. Eventually he found himself in a nice open space, larger than one might have expected from the house on the outside, a combined kitchen and living room complete with a flat screen television and a brick fireplace. "Would you like a drink?" she called out from the kitchen area, already picking out two glasses and the necessary bottles.

Preston stood and stuffed his hands in his pockets as his eyes wandered around the living room, basking in it all. "You know, you text nothing like you look," he called back.

She was silent until she emerged from the kitchen and handed Preston his scotch and soda, a glass of red wine in her other hand. "Most people just say, 'You have a lovely home.'" She walked past Preston and out the open sliding door onto the patio.

"It's a bit uh…" he waved his hand that wasn't holding his drink around for a moment, as if grasping for the right word, while he followed her outside, "bourgeois for my taste."

"Oh, so that studio apartment you share is a stylistic choice, then?" She took a seat on a corner of a sectional lying in the shade of a palm tree.

"Well, you know, it's actually a one bedroom, and uh…" Preston fell into the opposite side of the sectional, "not necessarily, but it does me fine."

"Oh, well then, maybe it's best if you just go back to it."

Preston took a gulp of his drink and shook his head slowly. "I can't do that." She scoffed and looked off into the distance beyond the lush backyard but didn't say anything. "I'm surprised that you're not surprised to see me."

She closed her eyes and rubbed her brow as if dispelling a headache. "I knew the mistake I made the moment I gave you my real name. Frankly, I'm only surprised it took you this long to track me down, I figured you'd be here that night."

"Well, there was a… a brief period of just kind of wallowing in self-pity before I started… researching."

"Oh, I think that period was anything but brief."

"Oh really?"

"Yeah, yeah," she nodded and turned her gaze back to Preston, "and I think it's still ongoing."

"No, no, not anymore. I'm done with all that."

"And yet, here you are."

"So here I am." He leaned forward with his elbows on his knees and his drink hanging in his hands in front of him. He peered at the glass surface of a nearby coffee table. "Do you have a coaster?"

She scowled at him. "Preston-" "Wouldn't want to leave a ring on this beautiful table."

"What are you-?"

"I know I'm not exactly a neat freak or anything, but I don't know, even I hate those rings. They're just... nasty"

"If you don't mind my asking, why exactly are you here?" Before Preston could begin, she interrupted. "I mean, I know why you're here, but what exactly are you expecting to happen right now? What do you think that this is?" Again, Preston tried to begin but she stopped him. "This is your grand, final gesture to woo me, I suppose."

"You could say that, I guess."

"Well, I'm going to tell you something that I think you need to hear, Prest-"

"Oh, please do," he said over a sip.

"Life isn't a fucking romantic comedy. You're not the main character and you don't get the girl as a reward just because you're at the end of the story."

"Right on, right on. I just think, you know, if I want the girl and she wants me, then it really only makes sense..."

"The problem with that is that the girl doesn't want you."

"I just think it's interesting that you chose to give me your name."

She threw her head back and let out a soft chuckle and a sigh before bringing it back down. "So, what, you think it was a Freudian slip or something?"

"I just said it was interesting is all."

"For someone who seems to hate themselves so much, you really are a self-important jackass."

"Come on, Dal-"

"Don't say that name."

"Sorry. Force of habit." A cool breeze smacked Preston in the face.

"I'm not just gonna drop everything to run off with some 20-something like I'm having some kind of... midlife crisis."

"What do you have to lose?"

Again, she scoffed. "My house, my fucking life, my marriage-"

"Ah, right, you're miserable fucking house and your miserable fucking life and your miserable fucking marriage."

"My marriage is not miserable."

"Quit lying to yourself."

"I have been married for eight years-"

"And you had an affair with a random guy you met over the phone."

"I didn't have an affair." She had started shouting, then nervously glanced around the yard as if searching for eavesdroppers.

"Would your husband say the same thing if he knew?"

"I love him."

"Then why did you need me?"

"Because- because-" she couldn't look at him now, and her gaze turned to the stone tile of the patio floor.

"Yeah, spit it out."

"Because we have our ups and our downs and because I'm fucking terrified of being alone and I wanted an escape. That's all you were, a fantasy that I used to escape my own shit. You didn't mean anything more to me than one of my novels. And now it's too real and I just- I need you to just leave."

"If you're so scared of being alone, then why won't you come with me?"

"Because this is something real," she said, vaguely waving her hands to indicate everything around them. "My marriage is something real, something solid, eight fucking years solid."

"And what makes this so real? Why is this more real than what we had? Because you're a fucking housewife?"

"I work from home," she tried to interrupt.

"Because you have... a fucking... a Mercedes and a pool and a lovely home and-" Another breeze rammed into them and tossed Preston's dreads into a frenzy.

"What makes it real is that I'm here, me, not Dalia Peterson, and I can talk to other people that are here and I can touch them and I can look in their eyes-"

"You said it yourself, we were perfect strangers, and that meant that we told the truth." Preston ran a hand through his hair, trying to make order out of it again. "That we were real. This is all fake."

"I didn't tell you that I was married. I didn't tell you that I was me."

"You didn't have to, that doesn't matter. You were you, really you, and I was really me for the first time- the first time since-"

"Since what?" He didn't answer. She set aside her glass and sat forward, staring him down. "Since Ophelia died." He stayed silent and looked down at his glass as he ran his thumb over its rim. She leaned back again, not looking away from him. She pointed at him after a moment, "You haven't cut your hair."

"What?" He brought his gaze back up to her.

"You still haven't cut your hair. After all this time, after you fell in love with Dalia Peterson."

He simply stared for a moment, then shrugged. "I don't- I didn't know any fucking barbers along the way, I'm sorry-"

"No, you're still in mourning."

He hesitated. "Maybe I am, but-"

"And you expect me to save you."

"Dalia, I-"

"That's all you ever wanted from me. And maybe you're right about me. I- I love my husband, but… I hate my life. I'm more well off than I could have dreamt of when I was a kid. My work is something I love and I'm good at it. I'm smart and I'm creative and I have disposable income. I'm married to a good man, and we have fights, sometimes bad ones, but I know he loves me. I have friends that like me and I like them.

I'm still young and healthy and attractive. And I hate my life.

"Maybe we wanted the same thing. Someone that would whisk us away and save us from everything. But that's not what real love is. Love is... a choice, not a feeling. It's doing all the everyday shit with someone. It's having the fights. It's taking all of them, not just an idea of them. It's not the grand gestures or the cross-country road trips or the happy endings. That's not anything real." her voice was soft, plaintive. So soft that he could hear a car engine abruptly shutting off outside. "And that's why you need to go home, Preston."

Preston licked his lips and swallowed back the tears he could feel welling up. "I can't do that. I can't go back, don't make me go back, please. We can go anywhere you want, just don't make me go back."

She shook her head and looked down at the floor. She couldn't meet his misty eyes. "I'm sorry that it had to come to this, Preston," she mumbled.

"I can't go back to Vermont."

"You have to."

"I'm begging you, don't make me go back. If you care about me at all-"

"It's over, Preston. I'm sorry it had to end this way. I didn't want it to be like this."

"Please-"

"I texted my husband as soon I saw that fucking Civic pull up my street. He's here, now."

"Did you tell him the truth?"

"I told him a truth." She finally looked at him. There were tears in her eyes too. "I told him you were a fan, a stalker, and that I was afraid of you."

"You were afraid?"

The front door opened. Echoes of footsteps flooded the halls, walking with speed and purpose. "Maddy?" a shout followed them.

"Out here, honey," she didn't take her watery eyes off Preston as she called back.

A man emerged from the house and stood in the doorway. His pale face was flushed with red and with sweat beneath his thick tawny beard. He was bigger than Preston, older than Preston, wore a nicer suit than Preston. "Honey, this is Preston."

The man was still for a moment, a savage look in his dark eyes. Preston couldn't get up out of his seat. He couldn't do anything. "I'm Preston," he announced against his will.

In a split second the man had launched forward, his leather dress shoes slapping against stone as he stumbled past the corner of the sectional and half tripped over and half knocked down the glass coffee table before pouncing on Preston.

Preston didn't really sense the fall. He heard her scream and he was just suddenly transported to the scalding stone ground, with the man sitting on his chest, crushing his lungs. He opened his mouth, but nothing came out and mere seconds later his entire being was jolted by a fist crashing down onto his face. Shock and adrenaline drowned all the pain, but he could tell his nose was cracking beneath the weight of the blow. The sun blinded him and seared his face. He reached a stiff arm up with no real objective, and felt his palm digging into the man's cheek. His pinky finger ran over something wet, maybe his mouth or maybe his eyeball. "Get the fuck out of my house," the man shouted as he brought another blow down. Preston felt the warmth of blood flooding his nostrils, he could taste it in the back of his throat. Water quickly filled his eyes and ran down his cheeks, mingling with the blood. He couldn't breathe, he couldn't see. He swung his arms blindly again, barely making contact with something fleshy. "Get the fuck away from my wife." Another punch. A third, or was it the fourth? Another. He couldn't count, he couldn't think. More punches, left, right, left, right, right, left, right.

He didn't know how many more punches came but it felt like an unending tide. Until he heard panting above him, then the shuffling of feet. The weight was off him, but he still couldn't move. That is, until he was grabbed by the tie and hauled off. Before he could know what was happening, there was a splash and then nothing. The heat was gone, the air was gone. The light of the sun warped and bended in waves. He was floating. He was drifting down towards the stone floor of the pool like a leaf drifts on windless air. She was gone, the man was gone. The yelling and the screaming were gone. The water and the chlorine tingling in his eyes were all there was. And he didn't try to swim.

But he was pulled. Some beast of the sea grabbed him by the collar and dragged him out to the surface, back into the heat, back into the noise. His back cracked on the patio and melted on the hot stone. He coughed and sputtered and cried until once more his throat was crushed. His tie was digging into his throat like a noose and once more he was dragged. The dragging didn't stop until his tie loosened around his neck, and the hand regripped around the collar of his jacket. One of his arms slipped out of its sleeve, but the dragging didn't stop. He couldn't fight, he couldn't claw at the doorway, he couldn't hold onto the carpets and the hardwood floors. for dear life. It seemed like only an instant before he heard a door swinging open and then he felt the blazing heat of the California sun again. The force dragging him continued for another instant and then tossed him forth like garbage, and he rolled first through grass and then onto pavement. He heard more shouting, but he couldn't listen.

Preston stumbled up to his feet. What remained of his suit was drenched and heavy on his weak frame, dripping onto the sidewalk. The man was some distance away, still shouting from the end of the walkway. The house's door was shut, and she was nowhere to be found. He took a few wobbly, hurried steps towards the Civic and got in the driver's seat. He wasn't really in control of himself, but whatever instinct that was compelled him to turn his key in the ignition and slam down on the gas pedal until the nice, quiet house in the nice, quiet neighborhood was far behind.

5

The rest of the day and the following night passed like a dream. Preston spent nearly all of it in the driver's seat of the Civic, cruising first all-around Los Angeles and then eventually breaking out onto the Pacific Coast Highway, floating across the coastal cliffs with the ocean right at his side the whole time. He had been heading north, but not to anywhere at all. It was night time when he got on the highway, and the light was just starting to come back now, the sky turning a pale creamy orange behind murky grey clouds. It never occurred to Preston to stop and get food. It never occurred to him to go to a hospital or address his wounds in any way besides the old rag from his glove compartment that he had held up to his nose to soak the blood for a few hours. It never occurred to him to go to the motel to get his belongings. All there was to do was drive. And he had come just as far west as he could.

Preston didn't concern himself with his mirrors, but when he did manage to catch a glimpse of himself, he saw the pale ghost of his own face with a bent, scarlet nose. Blood stains dotted the collar of his shirt. In the scuffle, his tie had come undone and now it was just a rope hanging around his neck. It was also flecked with blood, although it was nearly invisible on the black silk. He was still soaking wet, the steering wheel dripped in dew and the driver's seat saturated and decaying beneath him.

The narrow, winding highway was completely empty. The black asphalt, the cliff face it scarred, and the ocean that it loomed over were all washed in the glow of the rising sun. Preston kept a straight, blank face as his foot pushed harder into the gas pedal. The Civic's engine growled as the speedometer climbed. The rickety car protested with increasing volume as he pressed the gas pedal harder and harder as if he were trying to suffocate it. The speedometer kept climbing, the engine kept yelling. Turns became more difficult, he swerved in and out of the lines. He pressed harder. He wasn't breathing anymore. His chest was thumping, the beat echoing all the way to his ears, but he didn't pay it any attention. The Civic almost touched the rocky wall of cliffs on his right, or the sheer drop off the face of the continent to his left, but he didn't slow down. His tires were screeching, his engine roaring, echoing throughout the silent, barely conscious coast. There was a bridge coming up.

He couldn't brake.

He swallowed hard. He was rooted to his seat, his knuckles turned white gripping the steering wheel with both hands.

The bridge was getting closer.

He wouldn't make the turn.

Preston shut his eyes and tried to release the wheel, but his fingers wouldn't let go.

The Civic rumbled beneath him, he could feel it swerving on and off the road. Without thought, without hesitation, he wrenched the steering wheel to left and moved his foot to the brakes before pressing even harder than he thought possible. His eyes clenched shut even tighter. There was barely a second of mechanical screeching, of metallic screams before it all ended with silence. A wave of shock jolted the Civic and tossed him around in his seat. His head crashed into his window and then for an instant there was nothing.

Black.

What must have been a few minutes passed before Preston's eyelids slowly receded. More orange light of a rising sun flooded in and blinded him for a moment. What he first sensed was the feeling of floating nylon beneath his hands and his face. His sight returned to reveal that he was lying on the Civic's deployed airbag. He was fairly certain that this was the first time the ancient car had needed its airbag, and with it came a certain vaguely musty smell. He awkwardly tried to push the airbag down so he could look out the windshield. He found himself facing out towards the ocean, perpendicular with the white lines at the border of the highway.

It was at this point he figured that he hadn't yet died.

He moved the airbag around again in order to look out his window. He was just at the beginning of the bridge, the back-passenger's side door of the Civic completely crumbled around the resolute figure of the bridge's railing. The rear tires were just barely still on the cliff.

Preston dug around with his left hand for a moment until he felt it grasp around the door handle. His door swung open, and he crawled out from underneath the airbag. On his way out of the car, he felt his foot kicking against something, and he looked down to see his phone sitting there on the floor. The screen had a new, deep crack across its upper left corner. He leaned against the airbag and blindly fumbled for a moment, running his fingertips along the floor before he felt the phone and grabbed it.

He collapsed as soon as he got out of the car and was forced to stand on his own two feet. His suit was dripping and left a splatter on the asphalt where he fell. Pain echoed throughout his entire body, a vague yet profound aching that caused him to wince with every movement. Still, he managed to get up and limp his way over to the edge of the bridge facing out towards the ocean. For a moment, he leaned against the railing and looked out over the edge. Then, he summoned up his strength to lift himself up to sit on the railing.

He looked down to see his legs dangling over a huge drop, straight down into a rocky coast with waves of the ocean beating down upon it. He didn't feel real, sitting there, at that height, after everything that had happened. His only tether to reality was the pain that enveloped him like a blanket.

He stared down at the waves, the cliff face that seemed to stretch for miles below him, the sharp, jagged rocks bathing in the pale blue waters and jutting out like knives. The weight of his soaked hair and clothes seemed to pull him down, tempt him towards the edge.

He stared for a long moment.

For a very long moment.

Longer than he knew.

Then, he turned his eyes to the phone in his hand. He pressed the home button and was somewhat surprised to see that it was still functional. It took him longer than usual to scroll through his contacts. At times, he had trouble reading, not because he couldn't see the words, but they became utterly indecipherable at moments. Finally, though, he found what he was looking for, and brought the phone up to his ear. It rang a few times. "Hey, Brett," Preston said into the phone, still looking off at the ocean. "Look, I'm-" he chuckled. "Yeah, yeah. Are you still in Anaheim?... How's Quade?... Uh, I'm not totally sure where I am right now, but I think I know how to get back to L.A... Yeah, yeah, I've got a room there, I've got to pick up a few things... I should probably go to a hospital actually... The Civic's pretty fucked too, by the way... Nah, it'll make it back to L.A. I think... Yup... Yeah, I'll- I'll tell you all about it... Okay, see you later."

Preston lowered the phone and ended the call. Once more, he spent a bit too much time scrolling through his contacts. He closed his eyes, bracing himself before bringing the phone back up to his ear. "Hi, Mom. Merry Christmas," he said, then he took a long pause, listening. "I know, I know. It's uh- It's kind of a long story. I'll tell you when I get home... I don't know, I might make it back for New Year's... Well, I'm, uh... I'm not in town right now, so... I know, I'm sorry. Look, I'm... I'm coming home." He opened his eyes and stared out at the horizon, bathed in the morning sun's glow. "I'm coming home... Hey, um... What was the name of that doctor you were talking about? The one in Montpelier?

THE END

About the Author

At the publishing of this novel, Aiden Blasi is a nineteen-year-old student at the University of Vermont, where he is studying English and Psychology. He is also a DJ at the university's radio station WRUV, hosting the show B.A.D. Music under the alias of Bill Nyehilism. Apparently, he considers himself some kind of writer, though this novel is his first major publication. You can find a live documentation of his declining sanity at his website, aidenblasi.com; on Twitter, @bill_nyehilism; or on Reddit, /u/aidenfuckingblasi. Please direct all hate mail to writingaiden@gmail.com

Acknowledgements

No one reads these, so I'll try and keep it short. The first set of thanks goes to Lisa O'Donnell, my editor, my creative consultant, my benefactor, and, coincidentally, my mother. Next, my father, Lou Blasi, without whom I would surely be unable to write or in fact exist. My sister, Sarah, who helped me design my cover and who I am today. E.J. Ouellette for his continued support and inspiration. My publicist, Skye Wentworth, who helped me turn this into more than an old file on my laptop. All my teachers and professors. All the friends who have put up with my shit, and all those who didn't. And finally, everyone who unwittingly were sources of my creative inspiration, of which there are too many to name: Frank Ocean, John Steinbeck, Angel Olsen, William Faulkner, Mary Shelley, Kanye West, LCD Soundsystem, the Lumineers, the Coen Brothers, Hannibal Buress, Julien Baker, Travis Scott, Danny Brown, William Shakespeare, and it just keeps going on.